Alison Roberts is a New Zealander, currently lucky enough to be living in the South of France. She is also lucky enough to write for the Mills & Boon Medical Romance line. A primary school teacher in a former life, she is now a qualified paramedic. She loves to travel and dance, drink champagne, and spend time with her daughter and her friends.

DR RIGHT FOR THE SINGLE MUM

ALISON ROBERTS

MILLS & BOON

Published in Great Britain 2019
by Mills & Boon, an imprint of HarperCollins*Publishers*
1 London Bridge Street, London, SE1 9GF

© 2019 Alison Roberts

ISBN: 978-0-263-08050-6

MIX
Paper from
responsible sources
FSC® C007454

This book is produced from independently certified FSC™ paper
to ensure responsible forest management.
For more information visit www.harpercollins.co.uk/green.

Printed and bound in Great Britain
by CPI Group (UK) Ltd, Croydon, CR0 4YY

For every mother (and father),
in recognition of the amazing bonds we have
with our children xx

CHAPTER ONE

'HAS ANYONE HEARD what's happening?' Laura McKenzie slowed down as she pushed an IV trolley past the central desk of Wellington's Royal Hospital's emergency department and then she stopped. 'Has the baby arrived yet?'

One of the department's consultants, Fizz Wilson, was in front of a computer screen, studying the lab results on blood samples. 'Last I heard, it's not far away. Maggie was almost fully dilated. When Cooper brings Harley in for his feed later, I'm hoping we can use my break to go and meet the new arrival.'

'Yes… I'm due for my break at the same time.' Laura nodded. 'I'll come with you.' Maggie was a close friend and ex-flatmate and Laura couldn't wait to meet her baby.

'Where are you off to?' Tom Chapman, the senior consultant in this emergency department, dropped a patient file on the desk.

'To see Joe and Maggie's baby.'

Tom's eyebrows rose. 'Maggie's in labour?' He was already scanning the board that provided the update of all the patients currently in the department, whose care they were under and at what stage of their assessment or treatment they were. 'I was working with Joe at the rescue base yesterday and he thought it was still a week or two away.'

'Nope. Today's the day. They headed into Maternity at about four this morning.'

But Tom didn't seem to be remotely excited and Laura could feel a slightly puzzled frown line appearing between her eyebrows as she let her gaze rest on his profile for a moment longer. She'd worked with this man for more than two years now but sometimes she had absolutely no idea what was going on in his head. He was a brilliant doctor, was warm and kind and completely trustworthy but, at the same time, he could be oddly reserved. Like now, when you might expect him to share at least some of the excitement of imminent parenthood to people he knew well.

Maybe he just had other things on his mind. Like how his emergency department was coping with the patient numbers and the levels of attention they needed. Laura brushed off an urge to reassure him in some way that, as always, he had everything as under control as it was possible to have it but a couple of seconds later she thought that it had been just as well that she hadn't said anything because someone would have blamed her for tempting fate as potential chaos broke out. An ambulance crew was rushing through the automatic doors leading to the vehicle bay, someone was calling for assistance from one of the cubicles and a cardiac arrest alarm was sounding.

Tom was the first person to put his hands on the trolley that contained a lifepack, airway and IV equipment and the drugs that could be needed to manage a major cardiac event.

'Where's the arrest?' he demanded.

'Waiting room,' someone responded.

Tom started moving. 'Fizz, take over here for a minute. Laura? Come with me. We can get there before the arrest team arrives.'

Abandoning the IV trolley, Laura was almost running to keep up with Tom's long stride. Expecting to see an elderly patient who had collapsed in the waiting room, it was a shock to find that the cardiac arrest button had been pushed for someone who looked like a child.

'Help…please…she's not breathing…' The distraught woman who had her arms around the young girl had to be her mother and Laura's heart immediately went out to her. She'd be this terrified, as well, if she was holding her son, Harrison, and he'd just stopped breathing.

'What's happened?' Tom eased the girl from her mother's arms to lay her flat on the floor and then he tilted her head back to open the airway. He put his fingers on the side of her neck as he leaned closer.

Laura was peeling open the pack that contained the defibrillator pads. She cut the neck of the girl's T-shirt and ripped it open to give her access to the point below her right collarbone and then lifted the hem to press the second pad on her left side. She noted the dramatic rash on the child's skin and caught Tom's gaze to make sure he was aware of it, as well. He was. Of course he was.

'She's allergic,' the mother was saying. 'To dairy. She was eating chips in the car and I thought they were the plain ones and they were safe but they weren't… someone had given her some flavoured ones. Ketchup.

She thought that was fine but we could already see the
hives starting to come up.'

'We've got a pulse,' Tom told Laura. 'But she's bra-
dycardic. Not breathing.'

He reached for a bag mask, fitted the mask over the
girl's face and delivered a breath. And then another.
But he was frowning and Laura knew why. This had
to be an anaphylactic reaction to an allergen and the
child's airways were swelling up and making it harder
to deliver oxygen. They needed to move fast or it could
become impossible to intubate and secure the airway.
The fact that the heart rate was already too slow meant
that they could be dealing with a cardiac arrest as well
as a respiratory arrest in a very short time.

Tom glanced up and this time it was him who was
catching Laura's gaze. It was another moment of silent
communication and something they were both so used
to now it took only a split second to have a question
asked and answered. This was a critical situation and
every second counted. They would be losing quite a
few of those seconds to take the girl into one of the resuscitation areas on the other side of the swing doors
but it was entirely possible that they would need more
equipment than they had in this trolley—like a surgical kit to perform a cricothyroidotomy if a tracheal
intubation proved impossible.

With no more than a subtle nod, Tom broke the
glance, scooped the child into his arms and took off.

'Follow us,' Laura told the mother. She had picked
up the lifepack as Tom had started moving and she
really was running this time to keep up with him and
not break the connection between the pads and the
defibrillator.

People in the emergency department stepped hurriedly out of their way. Laura saw the startled expression on Fizz's face and the way she signalled junior doctors to take over what she was doing. She was right on their heels by the time Tom put the girl down on the bed.

'Respiratory arrest,' he told Fizz. 'Anaphylaxis. Known allergy to dairy.'

'Has she had any adrenaline?'

'Yes...' The girl's mother was near the foot of the bed, her arms held tightly across her body as if she needed physical support. 'We used her auto-injector but...but it didn't seem to be working. When she started getting wheezy I just drove straight here.'

She was used to coping, Laura thought. Used to providing her own support. Was she a single parent, like herself?

'Laura? Draw up some adrenaline, please.'

'Onto it.' The personal connection Laura was feeling to this patient and her mother had to be put firmly aside as she focused on what she needed to do.

Other staff members were arriving now, including the two medic arrest team. Laura was pleased to see a new nurse beside their patient's mother, easing her to one side of the room, out of the way, but staying with her as she endured the terrifying sight of a medical team fighting to save the life of her daughter.

There was so much happening. Tom was intubating the girl, using a video laryngoscope so that he could actually see what he was doing amongst the swelling tissues. An anaesthetist who'd been on call for the arrest team was setting up the ventilator that would be attached as soon as the intubation had been successfully completed. He had a kit on standby for creating a surgical airway if the intubation was not possible due to the amount of swelling.

Fizz was working to gain IV access and someone else was setting up the bags of saline and the giving sets that they would need for a fluid challenge to combat anaphylactic shock. Laura administered the first dose of intramuscular adrenaline and then began sorting the other drugs that she knew would be needed. More adrenaline, to set up as an infusion if there wasn't enough response to the first doses, along with an antihistamine and steroids. She filled syringes and taped the ampoules to the barrel of the syringes to identify them. She was keeping an eye on the screen above the bed, too, so that she could warn Tom of any changes that could be significant, like a further drop in blood pressure or heart rate. This would become even more of a challenge if the heart stopped in the wake of the lack of oxygen from the respiratory arrest.

The tension was palpable and, at one point, Laura heard the stifled sob of the girl's mother behind her. She could feel a lump in her own throat. This was every parent's nightmare, wasn't it? She was going to hug Harry so hard when she went to pick him up after work today that she knew he would squeak and wriggle free, probably giggling or groaning at the same time, the way six-year-old boys did. In the meantime, she was going to do everything she could to help save this young life in front of them. The alternative was simply unimaginable.

'We're in…' Tom gave a satisfied nod as he hooked his stethoscope back around his neck after checking the placement of the airway. 'Now, let's get this oxygen saturation looking a bit better.'

'Heart rate's picking up.' Like Laura, Fizz was watching the screen above them. 'And I've got wide-bore access on both sides.'

'Let's start the fluid challenge.' Tom turned his head to where the child's mother was standing. 'How much does she weigh?'

'Um…she was about twenty-six kilos the last time it was checked.'

'And how old is she?'

'Nine. Nearly ten…she's always been small…'

Like Harry, Laura thought. He'd always been small for his age and a bit underweight, as well. It made them seem younger than they were. More vulnerable. She wanted to give this young mother a hug. To try and reassure her. She could actually sense the same empathy coming from Tom, whose face creased in an almost smile.

'What's her name?'

'Elizabeth. We call her Lizzie…'

'She's going to be fine. The immediate danger is over.'

'But she's in Intensive Care…'

'This is the best place to monitor Lizzie for a few hours. Just to make sure that everything's under control and the medications are doing their job.'

The woman closed her eyes as she nodded slowly. 'I can't thank you enough, Dr Chapman.' She pressed her fingers against her mouth. 'I feel like it was my fault. How could I not have noticed that the auto-injector was past its expiry date?'

'I'm sure that's something that will never happen

again. And you did exactly the right thing, bringing her straight to Emergency.'

'I could have lost her. I... I thought I had...' She had her hand over her eyes now.

The urge to touch this woman's shoulder, or hug her even, to provide comfort was so strong that Tom had to curl his fingers into a fist.

He didn't get personally involved with his patients. Or their families. If he did, he'd never be able to do his job well enough and doing his job to the very best of his ability was the most important thing in Tom Chapman's world.

The only thing, pretty much...

'Go and sit with her now,' he told Lizzie's mother. 'Or take a break? You probably need one after all that drama.'

'I won't be leaving her side for a while yet. It's you that needs a break, I reckon. You worked so hard to save my little girl.'

'It's my job. And my privilege.' Tom glanced at his watch. 'I am on a late lunch break now. That's why I popped up to see that Lizzie was settled well.'

'I hope you've already had your lunch?'

'Not yet. That's next.'

But he wasn't really hungry at all, Tom decided as he walked towards the café in the Royal's entrance foyer. It was often like that, in the aftermath of the adrenaline rush that came from treating someone so critically ill—even more so when that fight for life was on behalf of a child. All life was precious, of course, but children and especially babies were so vulnerable you couldn't help becoming emotionally involved to some extent. For some reason, the feeling of connection was harder to shake off after this case. Maybe that was why Tom gave in to the impulse to turn into the gift shop beside the café.

Ten minutes later he was standing in front of a door in the maternity suite of the Royal.

Hesitating...

He didn't actually have to go in, did he? He could leave his gifts with one of the nurses. He didn't have to prod that no-go area of his heart any more than it had already been prodded today.

But visiting Joe and Maggie as they basked in the glow of new parenthood was a friendly thing to do. A polite thing, and Tom Chapman was always polite. Manners that had been developed as a form of self-protection had evolved to be useful under even the most extreme circumstances and he'd learned that there was truth in the old adage to "fake it till you make it". Tom had faked it for long enough to have made it long ago.

So, with the string of the pink "It's a girl!" balloon in one hand and the softest baby toy the gift shop had had available, Tom tapped on the door and poked his head through the gap.

'I can come back later,' he offered. 'If you've had too many visitors already.'

'No, come in, Tom.'

'Just for a minute, then.' Tom shook the outstretched hand of the paramedic who had become a trusted colleague in recent months. 'Congratulations, Joe. And there you were telling me only yesterday that you thought this was a week or two away.'

'Bella had other ideas.' It was Maggie who spoke.

'I have a feeling we're going to be scrambling to keep up with this little one.'

Tom smiled at Maggie, another paramedic who worked at the Aratika Rescue Base. Her blonde curls looked a little tangled and she looked exhausted but the glow of joy in her eyes nearly blinded Tom.

He'd seen that look before.

He'd worn it on his own face, once.

And yes…it was hard to drop his gaze to the bundle in Maggie's arms. To the tiny, slightly scrunched-up face of a baby who'd been born within the last few hours. The pain never really went away, did it? You'd think it had faded or been safely locked away somewhere but sometimes all it took was something like seeing that tiny starfish hand poking up from out of the blanket folds and there it was again. So sharp, it could have been yesterday.

So poignant, it could have brought the sting of tears if he'd allowed it. But, of course, that was never going to happen.

'Would you like to hold her?' Maggie offered.

'Ah…no…' Tom actually took a step backwards. 'I really can't stay. We're pretty busy in Emergency.'

He knew Joe was watching him. He also realised that Joe had respected the confidence of a personal discussion they'd had a while back now. That he hadn't even told Maggie that he'd learned something about Tom that he never told others. And Tom could feel the understanding in that gaze he was under. Joe knew that this was tough. That being with a couple who were so much in love and welcoming their first child had to be a painfully sharp reminder that he'd lost his own wife and son.

He didn't want that understanding. Or rather, he didn't want anybody feeling sorry for him because he had no desire to start feeling sorry for himself.

But Joe was nodding as he spoke. 'We heard about the anaphylactic shock you guys had to deal with. Fizz said it was touch and go for a while there.'

'It was. I've left her in charge, too, and it's about time she went home.'

'Did Laura come back? With Harry?'

Tom had his hand on the door already, but he turned back. 'Harry? Her little boy?' He was frowning. 'I didn't realise she'd gone anywhere.'

'She got a call from Harry's school and she had to go and pick him up because he was feeling sick. It's been happening quite a bit lately. If you see her, tell her to text me? She said she'd take him to the GP but if she was really worried, she said she might bring him in to see you.'

'Oh?' Tom shook his head. 'I'm not a paediatrician. I'm sure her GP can handle it. Or refer her. Laura knows that Emergency is just for emergencies.'

Laura knew she was bending the rules.

Okay, so a lot of people came to the emergency department when they had problems that could—and should—be dealt with by a general practitioner. And the fact that people did turn up when they had a minor injury or illness could mean that the department could get overloaded and the patients that really needed the attention of the staff might have to wait too long or even miss getting a critical treatment in time.

But this was Harrison—Laura's precious little boy.

And something wasn't right.

He'd had tummy aches before. He'd been sick at school more than once in recent months but there'd been something about him, when Laura had arrived at the sick bay to collect Harry today, that had sent a chill trickling down her spine. Maybe it was his skin colour. Or the air of listlessness about him. Or perhaps it was just the expression in those dark brown eyes he'd inherited from her. A sad look, as if he couldn't understand why life was so miserable right now.

Anyway, it was done. Laura was back at the Royal and had Harry in her arms, balanced on her hip. She was still in her scrubs with her official lanyard on so nobody would question her presence in the department and, technically, she was still on duty so she could tell people she'd come back to finish her shift and Harry was just going to wait quietly for her in the staffroom.

But the first person she encountered was Tom and the way he held her gaze for a moment or two longer than you would with a normal acquaintance provided one of those lightning-fast, telepathic conversations.

You're worried about your boy, aren't you?

Yes.

Too worried to go to your GP?

Yes.

Okay, then...that's fine...you've done the right thing bringing him in.

The lines around Tom's eyes softened and Laura felt herself relax just a little thanks to that understanding and trust in her judgement she could see in Tom's face.

She trusted him just as much and it was a trust that was rock solid because it had grown slowly to begin with when Tom had begun working in this emergency department. On both sides.

Laura was always wary around men she didn't know, especially when they were single and as good looking as Tom Chapman was. She had to make sure they got very clear signals that she wasn't interested in being anything more than a colleague. That she didn't want anyone trying to get close. It hadn't taken long to realise that the new consultant was giving off exactly the same signals but that hadn't stopped almost every other single woman she'd seen him interact with trying to catch his attention. A sympathetic glance on one occasion had cemented the unspoken knowledge that, for whatever reason, they had both built solid barriers to protect themselves.

Maybe that was what had given the level of trust between them such a solid foundation—that they both recognised those barriers and knew that neither was going to attempt breaking through them. They were workmates. Not quite friends, because they didn't choose to spend any time away from work together, like Laura did with Maggie and Joe and Fizz and Cooper, but they were more than simply workmates because there was that trust on both sides. That confidence that it was totally safe to be near each other. And that meant they didn't have to be on their guard on any level, which was probably why it was so easy to communicate, even without any words.

'Let's find him a cubicle,' Tom said. 'You fill in the paperwork and I'll come and check on him as soon as I can.'

He smiled at Harry before he turned away. 'Hey, buddy...who have you got there? T Rex?'

Harry clutched his plastic dinosaur more tightly to his chest and curled closer to his mother. Laura could feel the sudden tension in his small body from being too close for comfort to a man he didn't know. But her heart squeezed hard when her son was brave enough to say something back to Tom.

'His real name is Tyrannosaurus Rex,' Harry whispered.

'It is,' Tom agreed. 'Did you know that he had sixty teeth? And they were all razor sharp and could be this big?' He held his hands with a large gap between them.

Harry's eyes widened and his jaw dropped. Laura grinned at Tom. *Way to go*, she told him silently. He had just won the heart of a six-year-old who was passionate about dinosaurs and he might have even erased much of the fear that this small boy had of men he didn't know well.

She headed towards the central desk, to pick up the forms she needed to fill in and to check the board to see what cubicle might be free.

Fizz was on her way out of the department. 'Oh, no... Harry... Are you still feeling sick, sweetheart?'

Harry nodded.

Fizz caught Laura's gaze. 'Want me to stay? Cooper's just gone with Harley to get the car but we could come back.'

'No...we're good.'

Fizz raised an eyebrow. She knew that Harry was shy with men he didn't know. She also knew that her husband had won Harry's trust very early on, when he'd been one of Laura's flatmates.

'You remember Cooper, don't you, Harry? He helped you when you broke your arm last year.'

Harry nodded.

'It's all better now, isn't it? Your arm?'

Harry nodded again.

'Well, Doctor Tom will help make whatever it is that's making you feel sick all better, too.'

'He will,' Laura agreed. 'And who knew that he knew so much about dinosaurs?'

Fizz chuckled. 'There you go. A match made in heaven.' But her smile faded as she looked back at Laura. 'Text me,' she said, 'if there's anything I can do to help.'

'I'm sure we'll be fine,' Laura told her. 'You go and enjoy the rest of your day with your boys. I'm probably overreacting.'

'I'd be exactly the same with Harley. And we both know that you need to listen when a mum's feeling worried. Instinct should never be ignored.'

'Mmm…' But Laura didn't want to think about a mother's instinct. Because hers was trying to send messages that were too scary.

She just knew too much. She'd seen too much in this department. People that came in, occasionally, with symptoms that should be of no great significance but turned out to be something really awful.

Laura collected the paperwork and settled Harry onto the bed in a spare cubicle. She left the curtain open enough to be able to see what was happening in the department because she wanted to see the moment Tom started heading in their direction.

She wanted him to come and make her feel safe.

More than anything, she needed the reassurance that Harry was safe.

Tom collected the new patient file from the central desk and was reading through the information Laura had provided about Harry as he walked to their cubicle. Perhaps that was why it came as a bit of a shock to look up and see Laura and Harry through the gap in the curtains.

He saw Laura McKenzie almost every day he was at work but he'd never seen her looking like this. She was normally on her feet and always busy, caring for her patients or fully involved in an assessment or resuscitation scene. Even if she was taking a break, she'd be reading while she ate a sandwich, or chatting to one of her friends like Fizz.

Right now, however, she was half on the bed with her son, perched on one side and lying across the pillows so that Harry was tucked under the shelter of her arm. She was gently smoothing the dark spikes of his hair, quietly watching as Harry made his plastic dinosaur hop slowly across the blanket she had tucked around him.

Tom had never seen Laura staying this still, her body language shouting its focus on only one thing—her precious son. Or with an expression like that on her face. That mix of tenderness and concern—the picture of a mother's love—hit him like a punch in the gut and Tom found himself swallowing hard. To get a flashback twice in one day was more than a little disturbing when he'd been so sure he was well past that part of his life. Or perhaps this was simply an aftershock of how he'd felt seeing Maggie and Joe with their newborn baby and getting dragged back into the past like that.

It felt like longing, this sharp twinge of discomfort.

Or a renewed flash of grief for a future that was never going to happen.

Whatever it was, he knew he could handle it but it

was certainly giving him a new perspective on this woman he'd worked with for so long. Someone he had learned to trust because she'd never attempted to get past the guardrails he had in place in his personal life. And, in this moment, he felt closer to her than he ever allowed himself to get to a colleague or a member of a patient's family, for that matter. It was already under his skin. That note of tenderness. The knowledge that Laura was very vulnerable right now. All he could do was try and contain it. To make sure it didn't grow any stronger.

'Hey…' Tom pasted a smile on his face as he pulled the curtain shut behind him. 'How's it going in here? Is Tyrannosaurus Rex finding enough to eat?'

Harry hid his toy under the blanket. 'He's not hungry.'

'Oh…' Tom pulled out a chair and perched on the edge of it, so that he wasn't looming over the bed. 'How 'bout you, Harry? Are you hungry?'

Harry shook his head. 'I was sick,' he told Tom. 'At school. I was sick on the mat at story time.'

'Oh, no…' Tom could feel Laura's gaze on his face but he kept his gaze on his young patient. 'And you've got a sore tummy, too, I hear.'

Harry was silent. His chin was going down and his head tilting further into the crook of Laura's elbow.

Tom raised his glance. 'How long has the cream been on his arm?'

Laura touched the clear plastic cover that was keeping the generous blob of anaesthetic cream in place over the easiest vein to get a blood sample from. 'Needs another ten minutes or so.'

'Okay. So, tell me about what's been happening. This isn't the first time for a sore tummy, is it?'

Laura shook her head. 'It's been happening off and on for a long time. Almost since he started school, which made me think it was an anxiety thing, you know? Not wanting to go to school? The vomiting is more recent, though.'

'What's vomiting?'

'Being sick, sweetheart. It's what we call it here.'

Tom was watching closely as Harry looked up at his mother when he asked the question. Was that a tinge of yellow he could see in the whites of Harry's eyes?

'Can I have a look at your tummy, Harry? Is that okay?'

He could see the visible shrinking back further into his mother's arms but, with Laura's encouragement and reassurance, Harry let the blanket get pushed back and his tummy exposed.

'I won't hurt you,' Tom promised. 'If it's really sore, you tell me and I'll stop.' He eyed the dinosaur in Harry's hand. 'Or T Rex can bite me on my arm, okay?'

Big, brown eyes looked up at him. Exactly like his mother's eyes, Tom thought. Harry hadn't inherited Laura's auburn hair, though. The ruffled spikes of Harry's hair were very dark, almost black, which could be contributing to how pale that little face was. There was a hint of a smile there now, however.

''Kay.' He lay back but kept the toy dinosaur in a raised hand, ready to strike if it became necessary.

Tom was as gentle as possible. His hand looked so large against Harry's abdomen as he carefully palpated each quadrant. He left the upper right quadrant till last, probably because he had that suspicion of possible jaundice at the back of his mind.

'Can you take a big breath in for me, Harry? Like this?' Tom demonstrated and Harry complied.

And there it was...

A firm, irregular edge to this little boy's liver as he could feel it coming down with the lungs filling.

'Ow...' The plastic dinosaur tapped against Tom's arm.

'Sorry, buddy.' Tom lifted his hand but his heart was sinking. That prickle at the back of his neck was something he recognised all too easily and it came from the instinct that there was something significantly wrong here. That Harry could be in trouble and it might be impossible to protect him from painful things to come. Pain that would be felt by his mother, as well.

Tom didn't dare catch Laura's gaze just then. He didn't want to scare her. Not until he was sure about what his instincts were telling him. Maybe he just wanted to put that moment off for as long as possible because he knew, all too well, how it could turn your world inside out and upside down.

Destroy it even...

Or maybe it was because he was suddenly aware of a desire to protect Laura McKenzie.

Where on earth had that come from...?

CHAPTER TWO

THE REST OF that day became a blur.

A desperate attempt for Laura to hang onto something solid enough to not allow herself to get swamped by a terror that was becoming more and more real as the minutes and then hours ticked past.

Blood tests came next for Harry and they were still distressing despite the anaesthetic cream and how brave her little boy was being. Maybe it was so distressing for Laura *because* of how brave Harry was being. Her love for him was so huge, it was filling her chest to an extent that made it seem very hard to breathe.

There was an ultrasound after that and even though Laura was not trained to interpret the blobby images on the screen, she could see that there was something in Harry's liver that shouldn't be there. That was when the real fear kicked in. Fear that had to be hidden from Harry because Laura knew how sensitive he was to how his mother felt. He had been right from when he was a tiny baby and Laura still felt guilty that his fear of strange men had been instilled in that part of his life due to the aftermath of the trauma from the abusive relationship she had escaped.

Thank goodness Tom was there, at least until Harry was admitted for the raft of other tests he was going to need. It was Tom who introduced Laura and Harry to Suzie, a paediatric surgeon who was absolutely lovely, and he was there when the paediatric oncologist was also called in for a consultation. As Laura's world was being tipped upside down, Tom's presence felt like an anchor. Something safe when almost nothing else could be trusted any more. That something solid that she could hang onto.

'Can I call someone for you?' he asked when an orderly came to wheel Harry's bed up to the paediatric ward. 'Have you got family?'

Laura shook her head, stepping far enough away from Harry not to be overheard. 'No one close. It's just me and Harry.'

Tom was frowning. 'What about his father?'

'Not in the picture. Never has been.' Laura wanted to shut down this line of conversation. She'd been alone for a very long time, apart from Harry, and she preferred it that way. More than preferred it, actually. Changing it had never even been an option to consider.

'Friends, then.' Tom's frown had deepened. 'Maggie? I know she wants to know what's happening. She asked me to tell you to text her when I went up to visit her earlier.'

'She doesn't need to know right now. For heaven's sake, Tom. She's probably just arrived home with her brand new baby. It's okay, I can cope.'

She could. She'd coped before. Because, when you had to, you just did. You took things one step at a time and did your absolute best. But...it was kind of nice to have someone who wanted to help and the expression in Tom's eyes suggested there was something more than purely professional concern for her as a colleague. As she held his gaze for a moment longer, Laura almost had the impression that he was struggling with something. He felt compelled to offer assistance but he wasn't actually that comfortable about it, was he? Because they'd never stepped out of that "colleague" zone into a "friend" zone?

She needed to let him off the hook.

'As soon as Harry's settled, I'll pop home and get everything we'll need. And I'm sure it won't take long for him to feel happy there.' Laura pasted a smile onto her face. 'It'll probably be an adventure for him with all the toys and games they've got available and with other kids to play with and we both know how wonderful the staff are up there.'

Tom's smile only caught one half of his mouth. He knew how hard she was trying to make the best of this situation. He also knew how difficult it was and he wanted to be able to help. More than wanted, in fact. He looked as though he wasn't about to give up until he could do something. And, suddenly, Laura knew what that could be.

'I've got a day off tomorrow,' she told him. 'But, if you really want to help, could you look at my roster for the next few days?'

'Of course. Take all the time you need. Just let me know how I can make things easier.'

'Thanks.' Laura simply nodded. She couldn't spare any head space to think about how much paid sick leave she might have available. Or how much she had in her savings account to cover unpaid time off work. She did know that it was unlikely to be enough but that was an added level of fear that couldn't be allowed to matter at this point.

The only thing that mattered was Harry. Finding out exactly what was going on and how they were going to deal with it.

'I'll know more in a day or two and I'll come and have a chat about work then. It could be tomorrow, even. Suzie said something about the possibility of a biopsy straight after the CT scans.'

Even saying the words made the terror of this too real. For an awful moment, Laura felt an urge to throw herself into Tom's arms and just burst into tears. She didn't dare catch his gaze again now. He was feeling uncomfortable enough just offering personal assistance. Forcing him to offer comfort would be doing more than crossing interpersonal boundaries—it would probably irreparably damage the trust they had between them.

Those unspoken rules that had never, ever been broken.

No flirting.

No really personal conversation.

Physical proximity and touching only if unavoidable in professional circumstances.

Laura needed those rules to be in place just as much as Tom did because they were the perimeters that created the safe space she had needed for so long. It was a good thing that Harry's bed was on the move beside her. Even if she hadn't been able to control that urge to seek comfort from the touch of another human, there was no chance to do so right now.

'Mummy?' The anxiety in Harry's voice was more than enough to ensure that Laura took instant control of any emotional weakness that might be trying to persuade her to beg for comfort.

'I'm coming, sweetheart. Just wait until you see what they've got painted on the walls where we're going. I think there's even going to be some dinosaurs somewhere.'

Three days later, Tom emerged from one of the resuscitation rooms in ED to see Laura at the central desk. Fizz appeared to be hugging her friend fiercely.

He'd been expecting this.

He hadn't expected to feel a wash of something that felt oddly like relief at seeing her again, mind you. Had he been missing seeing Laura around the department more than he'd realised? Or was he feeling guilty that he hadn't been up to the paediatric ward to visit them? He'd felt a bit awkward, actually. Caught somewhere in the space between being simply a colleague or someone more like a friend who had good reason to demonstrate the kind of concern he was feeling. He had excused himself by keeping very busy and reassured himself that Laura was getting all the support she needed from her group of very good friends.

It was Fizz that Tom had been relying on for updates about what was happening in the paediatric ward and he always checked to see whether any extra help was needed. He knew that Harry had had all the relevant tests, including a biopsy. He had also been told that Laura was coping amazingly well, all things considered, and that she would be coming to talk to Tom, as head of department, regarding any time off she was going to need.

And here she was.

And, as Tom walked towards her, he wanted nothing more than to do exactly what Fizz was doing. To take Laura into his arms and give her a hug that could convey his empathy and encouragement and offer support all at the same time.

The urge to do so was disturbingly out of character for Tom. So much so that it was probably the reason he found it difficult to find a smile as Laura turned away from her friend. He might have even been frowning, he realised, as he saw the way Laura was collecting under his gaze as he came towards the desk. She was trying to hide any show of emotion that could be considered inappropriate in a work setting, wasn't she? Straightening her back and brushing both her forefingers beneath her eyes as if erasing any evidence of tears being shed.

She looked pale. So pale that Tom could see freckles on her nose and he'd never noticed them before. He could see stray wisps of hair escaping from the loose plait her long hair was in, as well, which was a far cry from the normally sleek way she tied up her hair, but what struck Tom the most were her eyes. Maybe she'd lost a bit of weight in the last few days, which made them look larger. Or perhaps it was the light she was standing beneath that made him notice the subtle variations in colour that made them a really golden brown.

No...in the moment Tom broke the eye contact before it became long enough to seem far more significant than it actually was, he realised it was neither of those things. It was the pain he could see in them that touched a part of his own heart.

He knew that pain.

He needed to straighten his own back now. To remind himself that just because he recognised how tough things were for Laura, it didn't mean he had to go back to that part of his own life and relive something he had finally moved on from. His heart sank a little, however. Even a professional chat with Laura was quite likely to be a lot more difficult than he had anticipated.

'This is good timing,' he said to her, by way of a greeting. 'Come into my office, Laura. Fizz? You'll know where to find me if you need me.'

'Sure thing.' Fizz had no trouble finding a smile for Laura. 'Come and find me again after you've had a chat with Tom. With a bit of luck, we can grab a coffee in the staffroom.'

Tom's office was down a corridor, between the staffroom and the meeting room. It was a small space, lined with crowded bookshelves and a desk piled with paperwork that took up most of the rest of the space. There was a big office chair behind the desk and two smaller chairs on the other side, which were padded but not exactly inviting. He waved a hand towards the smaller chairs.

'Please, have a seat, Laura.'

Closing the door behind him, Tom hesitated momentarily. Putting the barrier of that large desk between them didn't feel right but sitting close beside her on the other small chair was going too far in the other direction—as if he was planning to offer a counselling session rather than the kind of professional discussion about rosters and leave that they needed to have. He solved the issue by shoving a pile of journals to one side and hooking his leg over the corner to perch on the edge of his desk. Then he took a deeper breath.

'So... I heard that the biopsy results were going to be available today?'

Laura nodded. 'It's a hepatoblastoma. They thought it might be hepatic cancer because the age range for a hepatoblastoma is usually under three but...but apparently it's a good thing because the stats are better. The survival rate is...is around eighty-six percent.'

Tom used his nod in response as a cover to close his eyes for a moment. He could actually feel the strength that Laura was hanging onto as she spoke. This was her own child she was talking about, not a patient they had in common. How hard was it to try and focus on the positive side of the equation?

'And the MRI showed that there's no sign of metastatic tumours so that's really good news, too.' The wobble in Laura's voice signalled how hard it was for her to keep the lid on her emotions but she clearly wanted to give him all the information she could and Tom could only silently applaud her courage.

'Have they done the pretext staging?' The pre-treatment extent of disease was an important part of how the team would decide to tackle Harry's treatment.

'It's Stage two, but only just big enough to be in more than one section of the liver. They want to give him a few cycles of chemo to try and shrink it so that it's only in a single sector and then they'll be able to remove it totally with the surgery.'

'So surgery will be at least a few weeks away, then? Or more depending on how many cycles of chemo are needed?' Tom reached for a notepad and pulled a pen from the pocket of his scrub suit. 'Let me make a note of how long you'll need to be away for.'

But Laura was shaking her head this time. 'I don't

need to be off work the whole time. They're going to keep Harry in for a few days to see how he tolerates the first dose of the chemo but the aim after that is to keep life as normal as possible for everyone and they tell me that if Harry tolerates it well enough, there's no reason he can't keep going to school at the moment. Apparently most children do tolerate it well and he's desperate to get back to school and his friends and our normal routine. Hopefully I'll just need days off to be with him when he comes in for the infusions and I should have a calendar for that later today.'

Tom's eyebrows rose. 'You really want to keep working?'

'I realise that I will need a lot more time off when it's time for the surgery and that it could be a problem in the next few weeks if I have to cut shifts short or something to collect him from school if he gets too tired or is feeling sick, but it's not simply a matter of what I would prefer... I have to keep working, Tom. I can't afford not to.'

For a split second, Tom thought he had found a way to help Laura and still keep a safe distance. How easy would it be to offer to help her financially through this rough patch? Catching her gaze, however, he just as instantly dismissed the idea. He could read the look in her eyes just as easily as the kind of silent communication they could have regarding a patient. She didn't want financial help. She was fiercely proud of her independence and she intended to cope. Alone, thank you very much.

'We'll work around that, then,' he found himself saying. 'I know I won't be the only person in the department who wants to support you as much as possible, Laura. And… I have to say I think your attitude is…commendable.'

More like amazing, Tom thought. He'd always known that Laura was capable. One of the best nurses he'd ever worked with, in fact. He also knew she was totally reliable and trustworthy and, although he never listened to gossip, he'd picked up that she was a single mother. But he'd never put the pieces of the puzzle together, had he? He'd never wondered how she managed her life or how hard it might have been over the years. He knew virtually nothing about her private life and hadn't wanted to know. Until now…

'You're facing this head-on,' he added. 'I really admire your determination and how positive you're being.'

Laura looked down at her hands, which were clasped in her lap. 'It's not the first time Harry and I have faced a challenge. He was born nearly nine weeks premature and it was a bit touch and go here and there.' Her breath came out in a sigh. 'Apparently a low birth weight is one of the risk factors for hepatoblastoma. I'm glad I didn't know that at the time. I had rather a lot of other stuff to worry about.'

Tom was curious to know what that other stuff had been but stifling any questions was automatic. He hated people asking him personal questions so he'd always made a point of not intruding on the private lives of the people he worked with. Having this conversation with Laura was well out of his comfort zone and it wasn't just the subject matter. She looked different, being in civvies rather than the scrubs he was used to seeing her in.

She actually sounded different, too. 'I learned then

that you just had to get on with it,' she said, her voice soft enough to make Tom lift his gaze to catch hers. 'You get to choose some of the cards you play with in the game of life but others just get dealt out, don't they? There's nothing you can do about that except to play the absolute best game you can. And you have to fight for the people you love. For yourself, too.'

It was impossible to look away from those warm, brown eyes. She totally believed in what she was saying. Laura McKenzie was quite prepared to fight to the death for someone she loved. There was real passion there, mixed with that courage and determination. He was seeing a whole new side to the person he was so comfortable to work with and it was more than a little disconcerting because it was making him curious. Apart from being an amazing nurse and clearly a ferociously protective single mother, just who was Laura McKenzie? No... It was none of his business, was it?

The half-smile that tugged at one corner of her mouth made it seem as if she could read his thoughts and sympathised with his small dilemma.

But she was just finishing off her surprisingly passionate little speech. 'I guess that's the same thing, isn't it? If you're fighting for yourself that means you can't do anything other than to fight for the people you love.'

Okay... That did it. Tom had to back off fast before he got sucked into a space he had vowed never to enter again. He didn't want to think about what it was like to live in a space where you could love other people so much they became more important than anything else in life. That space that was too dangerous because, when you lost those people, you were left with what felt like no life at all...

He had to break that eye contact. And he had to move. Making a noise that was somewhere between a sound of agreement and clearing his throat, Tom slid off the corner of his desk.

'I'd better get back to the department.' He opened the door and there was an instant sense of relief. Escape was within touching distance. 'As I said, we'll work around whatever you need. Send me a copy of the chemotherapy calendar and I'll make sure Admin's on board for when you're rostered.'

Laura nodded as she got out of her chair. 'Thank you very much.'

Her formality was just what Tom needed to make things seem a little more normal. 'It's the least I can do,' he said. 'The least we can do. You're a valued member of this department, Laura. We'll all do everything we can to support you.'

Oh...help...

Where had that all come from?

Laura was cringing more than a little as she made her way back to the paediatric ward, where she'd left Harry happily watching a movie with his new friend, Aroha—a little girl with Down's syndrome who had been admitted to be reassessed and prepared for heart surgery.

Prattling on about playing the best game you could with cards being dealt in the game of life had made her sound like the kind of inspirational quotes that went around on social media.

And what about the way Tom had been looking at her while she'd been saying it all? She'd never seen an expression like that on his face. As if he understood.

As if that whole conversation had been very, very personal. That had felt weird.

Okay, Laura was well aware of how attractive Tom Chapman was. She'd heard plenty of women—staff members and even patients—who'd sighed over that combination of height, wavy hair, dark eyes and that killer smile. It wasn't just his looks, either. He had a way of focusing on people that made it obvious he was really listening. That what you thought or what you had to say was important.

That he cared.

Surely there wasn't a woman on earth who wouldn't have her heart touched by feeling that someone really cared. Maybe that was why she had stumbled into saying things that were too personal. Too emotional. For the first time, Laura had been affected by this man's personality on a level she'd never encountered before. She'd never thought of Tom as anything but one of the best doctors she'd ever had the privilege of working with. And a man she could trust not to come too close.

She took the stairs rather than stand with the group of people waiting for a lift to arrive. It could have been worse, she reminded herself as she began the climb to the third floor. She could have broken even more personal barriers and told him why Harry's premature birth and the months that had followed had been such a challenge—a fight for her own survival as much as her precious baby's.

It had been a long time since Laura had allowed herself to remember the horror of what had happened but it was inevitable that being on a staircase right now would set off those flashbacks she'd thought she'd conquered long ago.

The fear of believing that she was about to be hurt. Again. That the baby she was carrying could be in danger from its own father. Stepping back to try and find safety, only to feel that there was nothing beneath her foot, that she was falling and knowing in that same moment that the accusation that would come—that this was all her own fault—would certainly be true this time. Brent's voice when the paramedics had arrived.

'She just missed the step somehow... I tried to catch her but I couldn't... She fell all the way to the bottom of the stairs... Is she bleeding? Is she going to be okay? What about the baby?'

Laura's breath hitched as she pushed herself up the last flight of stairs. "The baby"—her precious Harry—had survived the emergency Caesarean and those weeks in the paediatric intensive care unit. He would never know about the night, just before he'd been allowed to come home, when Laura had stood up to his father during one of his alcohol-fuelled rages and threatened to call the police, and told him that she would do whatever it took to make sure her baby was safe from him. He had vanished from her life by the time she took her baby home and that was the start of a whole new struggle where Laura had to try and ensure that they both not only survived but thrived.

The early years had been incredibly tough but when she'd chosen to live with flatmates so that she and Harry weren't cooped up in a tiny flat and so isolated, life had settled into something that was as good as it could get, as far as Laura was concerned. Harry had been so happy at home, especially after he'd started at the nearby school. Laura had found great friends in her flatmates and then their partners, and had two jobs that she loved equally—being a senior nurse in the Royal's Accident and Emergency department and being Harry's mum.

Laura pushed open the firestop door in the stairwell and walked towards the brightly decorated entrance to the paediatric ward. Totally out of the blue, she had a new challenge that was every bit as terrifying as when she'd sat beside that incubator in Intensive Care, praying that her baby would make it. And yeah… Tom probably thought she was flaky, talking about playing the best game of life that you could with the cards you had been dealt and how you had no choice but to fight for the people you loved, but…those words of hers had been true, hadn't they?

At least Laura knew how to fight and that it was possible to win in the end.

She'd never been more determined that she was going to win a battle, either. Previous experience was helpful in reassuring her that she did have the strength. That, even if it felt like an impossible ask and you were on the brink of losing absolutely everything, you just had to keep going somehow—one step at a time—and eventually you'd find yourself on the other side. And it was going to be the winning side. It had to be.

For Harry.

And for herself.

CHAPTER THREE

THE FLUTTER OF excitement deep in his gut, as the helicopter skids lifted off the landing pad, was very familiar now but it would never get old. Joining the team at the Aratika Rescue Base as a HEMS doctor had definitely been the best decision that Tom Chapman had made in a very long time. You never really knew exactly what you were going to find at the other end of the flight, how serious the injuries or illnesses might be or what conditions you could have to work in to try and save a life. It was challenging, often thrilling and always enormously satisfying.

That disconcertingly personal conversation he'd had with Laura a day or two ago drifted into the back of his mind yet again but Tom found himself smiling this time. He *was* playing the best game of life he could, having included the extra dimension of his shifts at Aratika as a personal choice of one of his cards. And here he was, on a gloriously sunny afternoon, heading towards an isolated coastal area of the Marlborough Sounds—a beautiful area off the top of the South Island of New Zealand and only a short hop by air from the bottom of the North Island.

'Eighty-two-year-old patient who's fallen,' Joe mused. 'What are the odds that we're going to an NOF?'

'Pretty high,' Tom agreed. Fracturing a neck of femur in a fall was one of the more common injuries for elderly people. It wasn't something a rescue helicopter from Wellington would normally be dispatched to deal with but it was going to take too long to get any land-based local emergency service to the isolated area and a nearer rescue helicopter was tied up on another mission. 'With a view like this one, though,' he added, 'I'm certainly not complaining. Some people pay a fortune to see scenery like this from the air.'

'They do. It's stunning, isn't it?' Tom peered out of the window. 'Maggie's going to be so jealous when I tell her about this run. She's missing work.'

'How long till she comes back?'

'We're working on juggling rosters, maybe as soon as next month, so that we can share Bella's care. Cooper and Fizz seem to be managing well by doing that. They only need outside help with childcare about once or twice a week.'

'Hmm…' Tom was still focused on the pattern of green islands surrounded by deep blue water stretched out below. There were people living in places where the only access was by boat. He was only half listening to Joe as he wondered if loneliness could outweigh the peacefulness and beauty of the locations. Conversations about babies and childcare, or school, or whatever were so irrelevant to his life he often tuned out automatically but heard enough to make appropriate comments.

'We've got the advantage of having Maggie's mum wanting to help but I've got to get a spare bedroom sorted so that she doesn't have to travel late at night. And the place has been a mess ever since we started knocking the two apartments back into one house.'

'I can imagine.'

'Almost wish we had waited a while to start on that huge project. Maggie's a bit upset that we can't help Laura out at the moment and we could have if the place was still in two separate dwellings.'

'Sorry, what?' Tom turned away from the window, his attention suddenly caught. 'What's that about Laura?'

'She's going to have to find a new place to live. Couldn't be worse timing, could it, with everything else she's got to deal with at the moment?'

For a heartbeat, all Tom could think of was Laura's face when she had been looking up at him and making that brave little speech about taking the cards that life dealt you and playing the best game you could. About the courage and determination and...yeah...that capacity for passion that he'd seen in her eyes that had made him curious about the rest of her life.

He shook his head enough to clear that image. 'I don't understand,' he said. 'Why does she have to move?'

'She hasn't been able to find new flatmates and the house is way too expensive for her on her own.'

Tom could hear the echoes of Laura's voice from yesterday.

'...it's not simply a matter of what I would prefer... I have to keep working, Tom. I can't afford not to.'

That urge to help Laura kicked in with renewed force but, remembering how disconcerted it had made him feel to be aware of her personal life that had nothing to do with work, the need to keep his distance was already fighting with the desire to provide assistance of some kind.

Could he do something secretly? Like helping to pay her rent while she had to cut back on her working hours? No…he couldn't see how that could possibly work. If he had to make enquiries to find out who her landlord was, it was bound to get back to her and there had been a large element of independence as part of that determination to cope that he'd admired in her attitude to facing this crisis. Instinct told him that Laura McKenzie would not appreciate someone assuming they could undermine that kind of independence.

'There must be plenty of people looking for a place to live,' he suggested aloud. 'Has she put a notice up in the staffroom at the Royal? We could put one up at Aratika, too.'

Joe looked doubtful. 'I can't imagine she'd even want to be interviewing people at the moment. Or having strangers in the house when Harry's not well and facing surgery in the near future.'

'No… I guess not.'

'And I've always had the impression that it takes a while for Laura to trust anyone and there's not many people she lets get close. Maybe because she's super-protective of Harry.'

'Hmm…' But, again, Tom was thinking of the way Laura had been looking at him yesterday. Of the way they could always communicate so easily when they were working together. She trusted him, didn't she? As much as he trusted her. Perhaps that level of trust was even more special than he'd realised.

Andy, their pilot, cut into their conversation. 'We're

nearly on target. Keep your eyes peeled for an orange school bus on the road. It was the driver, Bernie, who called for help and he's stayed on scene. It's a fair way from any houses.'

'I can see it.' Less than a minute later, Tom pointed and Joe leaned to look over his shoulder. 'Three o'clock.'

'No powerlines,' Joe added as Andy circled back. 'But those trees look close and it's an unsealed road. We'll be throwing up a bit of gravel.'

'We'll head to that beach, I think,' Andy responded, banking the helicopter to the right. 'Looks like it's low tide and there's plenty of space. You boys will just need to get a bit of exercise and run up the hill.'

They didn't run, of course. You never ran when approaching any accident scene because that could interfere with taking in important details like any clues about how serious the situation might be and any potential hazards that needed to be mitigated. They did walk swiftly, however, especially when they heard the distressed cries of their elderly patient.

'That sounds like more than an NOF,' Tom commented. A hip fracture was often not particularly painful as long as the patient remained still. And these were the cries of someone who was terrified as much as being in any pain.

It was Bernie the bus driver who came to meet them.

'It's Maureen,' he told them. 'Ed's wife. She wandered off again and she must have slipped on the gravel and fallen over and hurt herself. He's having a bit of trouble trying to calm her down.'

'Wandered off?' Tom repeated. 'Again?'

'She's got Alzheimer's.' Bernie nodded. 'Should've

been in a home long ago but Ed's having none of it. He manages pretty well and we all try and do our bit but…' He was shaking his head now. 'This doesn't look so good.'

The frail, elderly woman was sitting on the side of the road. Her husband was trying to support her by keeping an arm around her shoulders but she was pushing him away, her frustration obvious.

'Go away, go away, go away…' Her voice rose as she saw Tom and Joe coming towards her. 'I wanna go home,' she shouted. 'I wanna go home, I wanna go home…'

Joe's glance was a query about whether Tom had any idea of the best way to approach this situation. He nodded in response. It wasn't that long ago that he'd attended a useful workshop in dealing with various forms of agitation, including that of dementia patients.

He crouched down in front of Maureen and mirrored her distress enough to let her know that he understood it.

'Oh, no,' he said. 'This is terrible. You want to go home, don't you, Maureen?'

She reached out to him, sobbing. 'I want to go home…'

'I know you do.' Tom took her hand in his and then put his other hand over the top of hers. 'I know you do.'

He started taking deep breaths and blowing them out in an exaggerated manner. Maureen was watching him. Clinging to his hand and still endlessly repeating her wish to go home, but she began to mimic his breathing pattern. Tom kept a hold on her hands, squeezing them rhythmically, like a slow heartbeat. Maureen's voice became quieter until it was little more than a whisper. Ed, her husband, was finally able to put his arm around her without being pushed away.

'Dunno how you did that,' he muttered. 'I don't think she could even hear anything I was saying.' He pressed his lips to his wife's silvery hair. 'It's okay, darling. It's all going to be okay now.'

Tom was still holding Maureen's hands. He spoke slowly and very clearly. 'Did you fall over, Maureen? Is something sore?'

She nodded. 'It's my leg. But it's better now. Can I go home?' She looked around. 'Where's the dog? I came out here to find him because he ran away.' Her head tilted up towards her husband. 'Who are you?'

'I'm Ed. I'm your husband.'

'I don't have a husband. Have you seen my dog?'

This had the potential to become a heartbreaking job, Tom realised as he saw a single tear escape and roll down Ed's face. Being able to distance himself by focusing on a clinical perspective was a relief. He turned to Joe.

'Let's get a set of vital signs,' he said. 'I'll keep holding her hands and talking to her and if you move slowly it should work. An ECG would be good, too. She might have had a medical incident rather than simply slipping on the gravel.'

Joe had been observing their patient carefully while Tom calmed her down. 'I can see she's got rotation and shortening on the left side,' he said. 'We were right about the NOF.'

Tom turned to bus driver. 'Can you go down to the beach, please, Bernie? We're going to need our stretcher. And an extra pillow so that we can splint Maureen's hip. Our pilot, Andy, will help you.'

'No problem. I'd better head off after that, though, if that's okay. Don't want to be too late getting all those kids home from school.'

Bernie was able to continue with his school bus duties and the decision was made to transport Maureen, along with Ed, to their nearest hospital rather than going back to the Royal. Well splinted and secured on the stretcher, with pain relief having been administered, Maureen was drowsy enough to sleep during the short ride to hospital but woke up as she was unloaded. Looking frightened and bewildered, she searched the faces above her and then saw her husband. She reached out both hands.

'Teddy...where am I? What's happening?'

He was at the head of the stretcher in seconds, leaning down to take her hands, to touch her face, to lean even further so that he could kiss her.

'It's okay, my love. I'm here. I'm looking after you.'

The look that passed between the two of them was something that would stay with Tom for ever. In that moment of lucidity for Maureen, he could feel the strength of the love they'd had between them. A lifetime of memories.

It had gone by the time they got to the emergency department of the hospital and handed Maureen's care over to the receiving team.

'I want to go home,' she told them. 'Please let me go home. I have to find my dog.'

Ed thanked both Joe and Tom for their help as they left a short time later. Tom shook his hand.

'All the best,' he said quietly. 'I can't imagine how hard this is for you.'

'They'll want me to put her in a home,' Ed said. 'But

it's not going to happen. Not while I've got breath in my body. And not while there's any chance of those moments.'

Tom nodded. He knew exactly what Ed was talking about. That moment of recognition. Of shared love.

'I heard once that dementia is the longest funeral you'll ever attend,' Ed murmured. 'But if that's the price to pay for all the good years we had together, then I'll pay it. They were worth it.'

Wow...

Tom barely registered that the gorgeous landscape below was even more stunning as the sun was setting on their journey back to the rescue base. His mind—and a large part of his heart—was still with his patient's husband. Thinking about how hard it would be to watch a loved one slip away like that but to still be living. He was also thinking about how many years the couple had had together to build that kind of a loving bond that meant Ed was going to fight to be able to continue caring for Maureen.

He was fighting for the person he loved.

Like Laura was fighting for Harry.

He didn't have anyone like that, Tom realised. Not any more. Nobody close enough to inspire the kind of self-sacrifice Ed was making to fight for his person. It made his life safer, certainly, but...

But, for the first time since he'd lost everything, Tom could feel the empty space around him. The loneliness.

What the heck was going on here? Had he spent the last few years since he'd lost Jenny and Sam in that horrific car accident too numbed by grief to feel things like this? Or had he built protective barriers that were somehow being undermined? There was a common element to the emotional tugs he'd been experiencing recently.

Laura McKenzie.

He felt too connected to someone who was facing the possibility of losing their son. It was her words that were running through his head when he was thinking about the battle Ed was more than willing to fight so that he could keep protecting Maureen.

'You okay, Tom?' Joe's voice almost made Tom jump. 'You're very quiet.'

'I'm always quiet.' Tom threw him a grin. 'Haven't you noticed?'

'True enough. Hey, are you coming to the training session tonight? The coastguard guys want to get us up to speed with their new boat and where to find everything.'

'Absolutely.' It sounded like the perfect antidote to any notion that the loneliness in his life might need to be dealt with. 'I was going to work on a paper but that sounds way more interesting.'

It was late by the time Tom was heading home after attending the training session but he felt good. He'd made the right choice in surrounding himself with base personnel and coastguard crews for the evening and it had been a great opportunity to get on board a rescue ship and learn about how things worked. He was going to keep his fingers crossed that he got a job with the coastguard before too long—like the one Joe had told him about, where he and Maggie had been taken out to a ship to rescue a fisherman with a dislocation and fracture of his elbow.

He was still imagining the excitement of getting out of the coastguard boat and onto a larger vessel in rough seas when he noticed he was walking past the gates of the Royal on his way back to his apartment. It wasn't that late, Tom thought. He might as well pop into his office and pick up the data he needed to start work on that paper he intended submitting to a medical journal.

It was quiet around the main entrance. A security guard stood just outside the semicircle of glass doors. He clearly recognised Tom but seemed to be undecided about whether to say anything.

'How's it going?' Tom asked.

'Fine,' the guard responded. 'For me, anyhow. I'm starting to wonder about her, though. She's been there for a long time. D'ya reckon I should find someone to go and talk to her?'

Tom turned to look in the direction the guard's head tilt indicated. He'd walked right past that figure sitting at the far side of the wide bottom step. Someone who was hunched over, with their head in their hands, looking utterly miserable. Someone with hair that had a reddish gleam to it under the artificial lights.

Oh... God...

It was Laura. And it looked as if she was crying. As if she'd been crying for a very long time.

'I've got this,' he told the guard.

He hoped he did, anyway. Despite his head issuing a warning about getting too involved, his heart was overriding the message. He could feel a misery that was close to despair hovering over Laura and it was touching him too close to his own heart. Tom had no idea how he could possibly help if Laura had had more bad news about Harry or something, he just knew that he had to try.

'Hey…' He sat down on the step next to Laura. 'I didn't expect to see you here.'

She raised a tear-streaked face, the expression in her eyes making Tom feel as if a giant hand had just taken hold of his heart and squeezed it hard. Then she groaned and scrubbed at her cheeks with her hands.

'Oh, no… I didn't want anyone to see me like this.'

'What's happened? Has something happened with Harry?'

'No…well…kind of…' But Laura couldn't say anything more. She just shook her head, squeezing her eyes tightly shut in an obvious attempt to stifle any further tears.

Tom tried to think of something that might help. Anything. 'Can I take you home? You must be exhausted.'

'I can't go home.' She was still making a visible effort to control her distress, gulping in some air. 'I have to go back to Harry but…but I can't let him see me like this, either.'

'Is he awake?'

'No…but…'

'You need a break. Coffee, maybe.'

'I can't go into the cafeteria. Not like this…'

'No.' Tom was aware that the security guard was still watching them. Other people arriving had turned to stare, as well. Whatever was happening for Laura right now, it was a private thing. She needed protection. That meant that taking her into his office where people from the emergency department could see her was also not an option.

'Come with me,' he said. 'I know where we can get a coffee. Not far from here, so you can be back in no time.' He held out his hand and tried to sound as encouraging as possible. 'Come on...'

She took his hand. He had only wanted to encourage her to get to her feet but as he led her away, Tom found she was still clinging to his hand. A bit like the way Maureen had clung to it when she'd been so lost and distressed. He could pull his hand free, Tom decided. It was quite possible Laura wasn't even thinking about any implications of the handholding, she was just needing that human contact. But he didn't pull it away. It was only a few minutes' walk to his apartment block, after all.

Besides, he'd forgotten how good it felt to have that comforting sense of connection to another person. He didn't really want to let go just yet.

It had been a lifetime since anybody had held Laura's hand.

Brent's grip had always been a little too tight. Controlling, even. But Tom's hand just felt...solid and warm. Protective. The way her own hand felt to Harry, perhaps, when she took hold of it to cross the road.

Whatever. The sensation of being led and not having to think about where she was going was a welcome relief in the middle of a meltdown that had happened because there were just too many things to think about and they were all just too big. Focusing on putting one foot in front of the other and the warmth of that hand holding hers was allowing her to step away from the overwhelming spin of her thoughts and it felt like that flood of tears was finally drying up.

Until she found herself going through an iron gate towards a small apartment block that clearly didn't contain anything like a café that would be providing coffee at this time of night. Confused, Laura's steps slowed and she pulled her hand away from Tom's.

'Where are you taking me?'

'Home,' he answered. He offered a half-smile. 'That's not a problem, is it? I thought you might appreciate a more private space. And… I can make good coffee.'

Silently, Laura followed him up some steps, through a front door and then into the door on the right. It was an old building and the apartment was spacious, with high ceilings and polished wooden floors scattered with rugs. Shelves overflowing with books and even a guitar propped up in a corner. It looked like a home, she thought as she heard Tom closing the door behind her. A place where a family could spend time together and relax. And, suddenly, that spin of scary thoughts sucked her in like a whirlpool and she burst into tears all over again. Silent, painful tears this time. She had to wrap her arms around herself to try and control the shuddering of her body.

She had her eyes tightly shut but she could feel how close Tom was. She would never have expected him to take her into his arms like that—not in a million years—but in the depths of the despair she was feeling right now, it didn't matter. It was just…so kind. Offering a whole-body version of that protective handholding. She wasn't going to fall into the abyss while she had someone hanging onto her like this. Letting her rest her head against his chest. Rocking her a little, even. Murmuring something soothing, although she couldn't hear the words, she could just feel the rumble of his voice beneath her ear.

She didn't wrap her arms around him—that would definitely have been a step too far but this seemed to be okay, even when she could feel Tom's hand moving in small circles on her back. It was simply one human being offering comfort to another.

The fact that she was beginning to wonder about how appropriate this was meant that Laura was finally escaping the whirlpool in her head. She could actually feel control returning, as if she was mentally pushing things into place and slamming doors. She moved physically, as well, and Tom released his hold on her body the instant he felt her muscles tense.

'Can I call someone for you?' he asked. 'Someone you could talk to, like Maggie or Fizz?'

Laura shook her head. 'I'm not going to disturb them at this time of night. If they're not asleep by now, they're probably wishing they were.' She tried to find a smile but she could feel embarrassment creeping in rapidly as she remembered where she'd been only moments before. Wrapped in Tom Chapman's arms? She'd never even seen him hug anyone. 'And... I'm sorry about that.' She looked away so that she couldn't catch his gaze. 'I guess it was just a case of the straw that broke the camel's back. I'm okay now.' This time she could find something closer to a real smile. 'Or I will be, after a coffee.'

'Onto it.' Tom's tone was brisk—as if he was relieved at the opportunity to change the subject completely. He walked towards the kitchen that opened off the living area. 'Make yourself comfortable, I won't be long.'

But Laura found herself following Tom into the kitchen. Because it felt like something was pulling her to stay close to him. A remnant of the comfort he had provided by holding her when she was crying perhaps. There was a table in the kitchen and a couple of chairs so she sat down and watched as Tom switched on a flash-looking coffee machine and then busied himself with coffee beans and a grinder. In a very short space of time, Laura found a very professional-looking cup of coffee being placed in front of her.

Tom sat down on the other side of the table and, for a minute, there was a slightly awkward silence between them.

'I have to apologise again,' Laura said, finally. 'I can't believe I cried all over you like that.'

'It's okay.' Tom was smiling. 'My shirt's almost dry already, see?' He patted his chest but his smile was fading. 'I'm just sorry to see you so upset. I wish there was something I could do to help.'

'You've done heaps. I might have sat on those steps for a lot longer if it wasn't for you, and you were right.'

'What about?'

'Needing a break. I haven't been outside the hospital buildings or grounds for days now.'

Another silence fell, less awkward than the first one. It was Tom who broke it.

'You've got a lot to deal with at the moment and it's hard to stay strong all the time by yourself. You've got some very good friends, Laura. Don't feel guilty about leaning on them.'

'Mmm…' Laura scooped a bit of froth from her coffee cup with the teaspoon. 'I can cope, you know. It's just been a lot of things in a very short space of time.'

'Joe mentioned something to me today. About you maybe needing to find somewhere new to live?'

Laura nodded. 'I'll get onto that. It's not a disaster—just bad timing. If I can find something I can afford, it would be so much better to move before Harry's due for surgery. That's if...' Oh, no... Laura could feel tears threatening again.

She picked up the teaspoon again and blinked hard as she focused on the froth still clinging to the edges of her coffee cup but she could feel Tom's gaze on her, like a physical touch. Questioning. Sympathetic. After his kindness, he deserved to know what had caused her meltdown, didn't he?

'I...um...had a meeting with the whole team this afternoon,' she said quietly. 'Our paediatrician, the paediatric oncologist, a radiologist and a nurse—even a social worker. I had a lot of questions, like what would happen if the chemo didn't shrink the tumour enough. If...you know...it didn't look like a complete resection was going to be possible.'

'Oh, Laura...' The tone of Tom's voice brought a huge lump into Laura's throat.

'They said I'm getting ahead of myself and that we can do several cycles of chemo, if necessary, before having to think about something like a transplant, but... I've been doing some research and if Harry needed a transplant I would want to donate part of my liver.' Her breath came out in a huff that was dangerously close to a sob. 'I'd give him the whole thing if that was going to save his life.'

'Of course you would.'

'But I can't even give him a piece of it and...and I think that's what the final straw was today. With my blood group, I'm not compatible.' She wasn't crying again. She wasn't. There were just leftover tears that were somehow sneaking down her cheeks. 'I'm A. I could only donate to types A or AB. And...and Harry's O. He can only receive a donation from type O.'

Tom sounded a little hesitant but calm. 'I know you said his father wasn't in the picture but...'

Laura shook her head. 'He's dead.'

'And his family?'

'They never knew about Harry. And I don't want them to.'

Tom still sounded calm. Reassuring. He wanted to help fix her problems. 'It might never come to that, Laura, but if it does, there'll be a donor available. I promise.'

Laura stared at him. A bubble of something like anger was forming in her chest. How could he make a promise like that? How could she keep trusting him as much as she did, if he was going to say whatever it took to reassure her when it might have absolutely no basis in reality?

'How can you say that? You have no idea whether that's true.'

'I can be fairly sure.' Tom held her gaze. 'I know there are other tests that need to be done but the first box has been ticked.'

'What are you talking about?'

'My blood group is O,' Tom said quietly. 'I'm a universal donor.'

Laura just kept staring at him. 'I don't understand,' she said. 'What's that got to do with Harry?'

'I'm saying that, if a transplant is needed at some

point in the future, I could do that. I could donate part of my liver to Harry.'

'Why?' The word came out as a whisper. 'Why would you do that for someone you barely know? It's not like donating blood, you know. It's risky. The kind of risk you'd take for your own child, but for someone else's?'

She knew she was searching Tom's face, looking for an answer. Or checking to see whether this incredible offer was genuine? Who was this quiet, clever man she'd been working with for so long? Laura felt like she didn't know him at all in this moment.

'Maybe that's why,' Tom said softly. 'I can't do it for my own child because I lost Sam a long time ago—in the same car accident that killed my wife.'

'Oh, my God, Tom... I'm so sorry... How could I have not known that?'

'It's not something I talk about. I find life's easier that way.'

The ground had just shifted beneath Laura's feet. He really did understand what she was facing. He'd been in an even worse space himself. She desperately wanted to reach out and touch him and her hand actually moved on the table but something stopped her. Perhaps it was because his words were personal enough and already breaking an unspoken barrier between them that made this space feel fragile. It felt like touching Tom when he was stepping into the new space for the first time might be enough to push him back into hiding.

'That's...unimaginable,' she said slowly. 'How old was he?'

She could see the muscles move in Tom's neck,

which made it look as if it was painful to swallow. 'He was two. And it was about four years ago so that would make him about the same age as Harry if he was still alive.'

Laura closed her eyes. She was thinking back to that conversation she'd had with Tom in his office that day. When she'd had the impression that he really understood what she was going through as she'd grappled with Harry's diagnosis and upcoming treatment. How personal it had felt.

Of course it had. He must have been struggling with his own memories of losing a child.

'I don't know what to say,' she said softly. 'Except that I'm so sorry that it happened.'

'Yeah…me, too.' Tom said. 'I'm used to life on my own now, but I still miss them every day. Jenny. And my Sam.'

It didn't seem to matter that Laura hadn't reached out to touch Tom in any way. The eye contact they were sharing was having the same effect.

Connecting them.

As parents. Acknowledging the depth of love you had for your child. As medical professionals, as well, knowing the lengths that you would go to in order to save a child's life. And perhaps there was something else connecting them now that had never been there before.

Something that had been born in that bubble of time when Tom had been holding her in his arms and letting her cry. Laura wasn't at all sure what it was but she could feel its presence. Something fundamental had changed between them. The barriers that kept personal things safely enclosed were shifting. Getting blurred.

It almost felt as if she and Tom were becoming real friends rather than simply colleagues but, on top of everything else she was grappling with emotionally, it was too much to think about at the moment.

'I'd better get back to the hospital,' she said. 'I don't want Harry waking up to find I'm not there.'

'I'll walk back with you.'

Laura opened her mouth to protest. To tell him that she was perfectly capable of walking by herself and to pull her cloak of independence more tightly into place, but the words failed to emerge. Because the cells in her skin were reminding her of what it had felt like when Tom had taken her hand as he'd led her away from the Royal's front steps. Of how protected she had felt when she'd been in his arms. Not that she was going to hold his hand on the way back, mind you, but if he wanted to offer his protection—how could she refuse?

It was heartbreaking that he didn't have the people he really wanted to protect in his life any more.

'That would be great,' was what Laura said instead as she got to her feet. 'Thanks, Tom.'

CHAPTER FOUR

NOTHING WAS QUITE the same.

On the one hand, it felt wonderful to be back in the emergency department of the Royal for the first shift that Laura had managed to roster since Harry had become sick. It was a slice of "normal" in a life that had been turned upside down and was still being shaken at regular intervals. More importantly, it was a slice of normal for Harry. He'd been itching to get back to school and see his friends and he seemed to be tolerating this first cycle of chemotherapy so well it had been decided he could try a return to school and he was loving it.

The staff of both the school and its aftercare facility were being incredibly supportive and, as she'd donned her scrubs and walked through into the working space she loved so much, Laura realised just how valuable this was going to be to her own mental health as a distraction from everything else going on in her life at the moment. She just had to try and put this new tension to one side so that it didn't interfere with her focus on patients—the tension that was caused by her half expecting a call at any moment to say that she needed to be with Harry because he had suddenly become very unwell again.

At least she could put it to one side here and she hadn't been able to do that at home in the few days since Harry had been building up the time he spent at school. He might have been out of sight for an increasing number of hours but he'd never been out of her mind. Not even for a minute.

She'd spent the last ten minutes focusing completely on six-month-old Alfie, however, and hadn't thought about Harry at all. She'd been too busy taking the baby's vital signs again and reassuring the anxious mother that a doctor would be available very soon to examine her son.

That it was Tom Chapman who came into the cubicle made Laura aware of something else that was different about being back at work. They'd always had a great working relationship and had been able to communicate so well that sometimes it didn't even require words, but it felt different now. He had done more than simply look after her the other night when she had been so upset. He had shared a part of his private life with her and, as far as she knew, he'd never shared that with anyone else he worked with and that made her feel trusted. Special.

And because of what he'd shared, Laura could now see Tom as a man quite apart from Tom as a doctor and trusted colleague. She could see him as a husband. As a father. As someone who had endured unimaginable grief. And as someone who had extended a hand of kindness to her. Quite literally, in fact, when he'd taken her hand and led her to his home that night.

Even more than any of that, he had actually offered

to get himself tested and be available as a living donor if Harry ended up needing a liver transplant. What kind of person did that? Someone selfless. Altruistic. Possibly the kindest person on earth so the warmth that Laura was feeling towards Tom was really not surprising at all. It was, however, a significant shake-up in her life on top of everything else. A not unpleasant shake-up, mind you. It was just that Laura didn't ever feel like this any more. Not when a man was involved, that is. A single man.

She'd never had the slightest desire to look for another relationship after Brent had vanished from her life. That was partly because her baby had become the centre of her life and she had told herself that was all she needed, but the real reason had more to do with the damage that had been done to her self-esteem. There were only so many times you could be told that you were stupid or ugly or that everything was your fault before you started believing it.

And, even if she'd had moments of knowing it wasn't true and of believing in herself, there was the inescapable fact that she had fallen in love with Brent and then stayed with him for far too long, believing in those apologies and promises that it would never happen again. It had been preferable to stay single than to risk trusting her own judgement when it came to men. Imperative, actually, because it wasn't just herself that she'd be putting at risk if she got things so badly wrong again and there was no way Laura would ever, ever put Harry at risk.

Ever since she had freed herself from her disastrous relationship with Brent, even an appreciative look, let alone an invitation for a date, had been enough to raise her hackles and prompt her to reinforce her protective barriers. Any attempts to let a friendship develop with a single male had always failed because they always ended up wanting more than friendship so it had become an automatic way of life not to let men close. It had been so many years since she Laura had felt this kind of warmth for a man that just thinking about them, let alone being physically close to them, could provoke, but she was feeling it now as Tom came closer.

Not that it was hard to hide it, thank goodness. This was a professional setting after all and, even if it wasn't, Laura knew that Tom would not welcome any move on her part to demonstrate her new appreciation of him as a person. She could actually sense the slight tension in the air between them, as if he was expecting her to do or say something unwelcome. He might have held her hand when she'd been blinded enough by her tears to not see where she was going properly, but there'd been a perfectly normal distance between them when he'd walked her back to the hospital. He wouldn't even talk any more about his offer of being a donor.

It might never come to that, he'd said. *So we don't have to talk about it any more at the moment and I'd really prefer it if no one else knows about this. Let's just wait and see.*

It was hardly surprising, though, that Laura had such a squeeze happening around her heart when she saw Tom being so gentle with little Alfie, as he took the baby from his mother's arms and laid him on the bed beside her. The knowledge that he had been a father himself couldn't be shut away and ignored.

'It's okay, little man,' he said. 'We just want to find

out what's making you unhappy.' He glanced over his shoulder at Laura, one eyebrow raised.

'Blood pressure, heart and respiration rate and temperature all within normal limits,' she told him. 'He hasn't vomited again but he was sick four times at home this morning.'

Tom turned his glance to Alfie's mother. 'Does he seem more lethargic to you at the moment? Is this his normal colour?'

'No. He looks really pale to me. And he's kind of floppy… He's never usually this quiet. And he was screaming his head off all morning. It sounded different, too…'

'In what way?'

'I don't know. Kind of high-pitched, I guess. As if he was really in pain. And he was pulling his legs up. I've read online that that's supposed to mean they've got a sore tummy. That was when I got really worried and decided to come here.'

Baby Alfie had caught Tom's thumb and wrapped his tiny fingers around it. Tom's face softened.

'Wotcha got, little man?'

He joggled his hand, which made Alfie's arm bounce and made the baby smile for the first time A toothless grin that made Tom smile back and Laura could feel another squeeze on her heart. He would have been like this with his own baby once. Delighting in every smile. Comforting him when he was distressed. Having dreams of the future when he would be playing with a toddler who was taking his first steps or a child who could run and kick a football or a teenager, maybe, who wanted to learn to drive a car. Dreams that Laura had had with Harry and she was still clinging to them.

She couldn't afford to let herself imagine how devastating it would be to have them ripped away from her, the way they had been for Tom. He hadn't just lost his child, either, he'd also lost the woman he'd loved enough to marry and promise to spend the rest of his life with. Laura's heart had been aching for Tom ever since he'd told her that small part of his story. How hard was it for him to deal with babies and children as patients?

He seemed to be coping just fine with Alfie. Enjoying it, even. He had retrieved his thumb and was gently examining the baby's abdomen.

'It's nice and soft,' he told Alfie's mother. 'I can't feel anything that could be a problem and it's not upsetting him enough to make me think he's in any pain at the moment.'

'He seems so much better,' she said. 'I hope I'm not wasting everybody's time by having brought him in.'

'Not at all.' It was Laura who stepped in to reassure her. 'We always take notice of a mother's instinct about how unwell her baby is.'

Like Tom had done that day she'd brought Harry in. In that last bit of time before her world had tipped upside down. He'd been so good with her little boy that day, as well, winning his heart almost instantly by bonding over dinosaurs. It said a lot about him that he could interact so well with his youngest patients. Surely there had to have been a time when it must have been the most difficult thing in the world to do.

'You did exactly the right thing,' Tom agreed. 'We're going to keep our eye on Alfie for a while and do some tests to rule out any kind of infection. I'm afraid that means a blood test but we'll be as quick and gentle as we can.'

'The anaesthetic cream has only been on for twenty minutes or so,' Laura said. 'It'll take an hour to be really effective.'

'Oh…okay. We'll leave it a bit longer then.'

Tom's glance told Laura that he wanted a careful eye to be kept on Alfie. Her smile and nod told him she would let him know if anything changed. It was a very familiar sort of communication between them.

But it felt different. Bigger, somehow. Special…

Well, that was a bit of a relief.

Tom had wondered, since the last time he'd seen Laura, whether telling her about his tragic past or making that somewhat impulsive offer about being a living donor for Harry would affect their working relationship in some way. He fully expected that it would, by giving them the kind of personal ground that he'd avoided so carefully for so many years with any of his colleagues. Even without inviting a woman to share any part of his private life, he was often on the receiving end of a look he'd come to know all too well. That invitation to share a lot more than simply a conversation. It would be such a disappointment if he ever saw a glimmer of that look in Laura McKenzie's eyes.

He'd shocked himself a little, to be honest, by making that offer of being a donor, but he'd given it a lot of thought since then and he hadn't changed his mind, even after reading up on the extensive check-ups he would need to determine his own state of health, the potential complications and how long his recovery could take. It still felt like the right thing to do because

Tom could imagine how it might have made the world a much better place if somebody had been able to do something to try and save his own son's life.

It wasn't that he was singling out Laura, or Harry for that matter, as being particularly special in his life, it was just that the opportunity was here in front of him. A little boy had been lost but he could do something to save another little boy. An act to balance a tiny part of the universe, perhaps, and move on with his own healing.

Quite apart from never wanting Laura to look at him with any hint of sexual interest, he didn't want her premature gratitude for something that might never happen, either. He didn't want her sympathy for the huge loss he had suffered in his life and he certainly didn't want her looking at him when he was dealing with babies and children and wondering whether it reminded him of what he'd lost. Of course it did at times. In the early days it had been unbearable but that was precisely how Tom had learned to control what he was allowed to think about and, more importantly, the feelings he was allowed to acknowledge. If he hadn't, he felt like he might not have survived.

It had been there the day that Laura had brought Harry into the emergency department here. And it was here, to some extent, when he was examining baby Alfie simply because of that background concern that Laura might have read too much into the fact that he'd taken her home to give her a break from the hospital. That he'd held her hand. And especially that he'd made an offer that was clearly above and beyond what most colleagues would do for each other.

But, if anything had changed, it hadn't made Laura

look at him in any way that had made alarm bells of any kind ring and that was definitely a relief. A big relief. She was looking a little more tired than usual, perhaps—and who wouldn't with the amount of stress she was still dealing with—but their working relationship appeared to be exactly what it had always been. They could even communicate by no more than a glance, like when he'd wanted to tell her to keep a very close eye on this baby but he hadn't wanted to alarm Alfie's mother by saying anything aloud.

She was there to hold Alfie's little arm still when he went back to take the blood sample. Working together on the delicate task of inserting a cannula into such a small vein and getting the sample they needed made Tom relax even more concerning their professional relationship and hopefully that would extend to any personal relationship, as well. Nothing had really changed. He could even dismiss that nagging memory of how he'd felt during that conversation in his office that day and that it could have been responsible for that new, unwelcome notion that his life was lonely.

He still felt safe with Laura and that was enough of a relief to put a smile on his face when she came into the staffroom just as he'd finally found a chance to go and grab a cup of coffee.

'Tom? Have you got a minute?'

He could hear the note of urgency in her voice and instantly abandoned his hot drink. 'Of course. What is it?'

'Alfie. He's clearly in pain again and I've just found a significant amount of blood and mucus in his nappy.'

'Sounds like it could be intussusception.'

'That's what I was thinking. Shall I get the portable ultrasound machine? Or call the radiographer for an X-ray?'

'Let's have another look at him. And chase up any blood results in case it's an infection we're dealing with.'

There were no smiles from Alfie this time, and his mother was looking just as distressed.

'He seemed to be feeling so much better...'

'The symptoms can be intermittent,' Tom explained. 'It's looking like this could be what's called an intus-susception. It's where a part of the intestine folds inside another part—like a telescope—and causes an obstruction.'

'Is it dangerous?'

'Only if it's left untreated, and the earlier we deal with it the better. There's an enema intervention that could mean he won't need surgery but I'm going to call a paediatric surgeon in for a consultation and it'll be their call what happens next. Try not to worry too much. I'm going to give Alfie something to help the pain and Laura's going to look after you until the pae-diatric team takes over. You're lucky—you've got our best nurse to take care of you both.'

Maybe the casual compliment had been a subcon-scious test. When he received only a subtle headshake and hint of a smile, rather than any significant eye contact, Tom knew he was right to feel safe. He had this—whatever it was between them that didn't quite fit within professional boundaries—completely under control. Okay, Harry—and his mother—had got under his skin more than he normally allowed because there was some kind of connection there, but he could still keep a safe distance. It didn't mean that he was making a big mistake in offering the kind of support that being a potential donor entailed. Or that he had to stamp on any urges to do whatever else he might be able to do to help Laura.

Yes, it had been disturbing, during that oddly intimate end to his conversation with Laura in his office, to feel that pull towards the kind of space where you loved someone enough to do whatever was necessary to fight for them. The kind of space he'd inhabited when he'd had his own small family and one that he had been quite sure he would never be in again. A space he didn't even want to risk getting close to because he never wanted to risk having to climb out of that abyss of loss ever again.

But keeping a safe distance didn't mean that he wasn't allowed to care a little more than usual in this case, did it? Or that he couldn't allow himself to be involved? He would know if he was getting too involved and then all he would need to do would be to step back.

Yep. He had this pegged. He was at a new stage in his life, perhaps, where part of him had healed. Or scarred over enough to offer him all the protection he needed. You could help someone build a house, for example, he reasoned to himself. You could even wish that things were different and you could live in a house again yourself, instead of being isolated in a small apartment. It didn't mean that you had to move in and live with them, however, and it would not change the knowledge of where you now belonged. But you could visit, if that person was a trusted friend.

That's what had changed.

It felt like he and Laura had become friends.

* * *

'They've taken Alfie to Theatre.' Laura was pleased to see that Tom had finally found a moment to make himself a fresh cup of coffee. She reached for a mug from the staffroom cupboard herself, dropped in a tea-bag and poured boiling water on top. 'I'll try and pop up to see his mum and find out how it went before I go to pick up Harry. How long will the surgery take, do you think?'

'That will depend on whether there's any intestinal damage that needs to be removed.' Tom glanced up at the wall clock. 'It could well take longer than you might expect. I was planning to follow up on the case myself. I can let you know the next time you're on duty, if you like.'

'That would be awesome.' Laura added a splash of milk to her tea and then sat down and took a sip.

'When are you working again?'

'Not sure. This will have been Harry's longest day at school today so I'll see how it went. We've got a session in the oncology day unit tomorrow for another infusion, too, so that might change things.'

'How's he doing?'

'Remarkably well. He gets tired and there are some foods that make him feel sick but the side effects are pretty well controlled. He is starting to lose his hair, though, and he's worried that the kids are going to tease him.'

'Hmm…'

It was no more than a sympathetic sound. Tom wasn't even looking at Laura when he made it—he was peering into his mug as if to check how much coffee he had left—but she felt the sound resonate as it travelled a lot further than simply her ears. She could feel it expanding inside her body and triggering one of those waves of warmth.

'Let me know if there's anything I can do to help,' he added. 'Anything at all, okay?'

The sincerity in his tone gave Laura a lump in her throat. This was getting a bit weird. Tom wasn't even a friend, really. She shouldn't be feeling this…close.

But then he looked up and there was something different about the way he was looking at her. They were so used to having those lightning-fast, silent communications about professional things. It wasn't the first time they'd had one on a more personal level, though, Laura realised. There might not have been clear words involved in the way he'd looked at her in his office that day but she'd been right in knowing that he did understand exactly where she was coming from.

And, way back, there'd been that time when they had first been working together when she'd let him know that she understood how much he disliked women coming on to him in any way and, in that moment, the trust between them had probably been born.

This message was something very different. It was acknowledging that they were closer than they had been but there was nothing remotely threatening in that look that might have reminded Laura why it never worked to be friends with a single male. He might be seeing her as more than a colleague now but it would never be as more than a friend. She knew he had his own safety barriers and she could be sure that they weren't going to be taken down any time soon, if ever. He had loved his wife and child so much he was still missing them every day.

She was still safe.

If there'd been a particular moment when the trust between them had been born, she might look back at this moment and realise it was when a friendship had been created.

One that felt like it could last a lifetime.

CHAPTER FIVE

THE RELIEF TOM had been aware of all day made him feel very content with his life as he finally clocked off and headed home after a visit to the paediatric intensive care unit to check on the excellent progress baby Alfie was already making.

As he popped into the supermarket for a few supplies, he reminded himself that Laura would want to know about the baby. He could tell Fizz tomorrow perhaps and she could pass on the positive result. Or he could even take a minute to find her in the oncology day unit, because it really did feel like they were friends now, and not just colleagues.

Perhaps it was making that mental note that made him think about Laura again, as he walked past the bargain bin offerings the supermarket had on display. Or rather it was Harry that he was thinking about now. After what Laura had said about him being worried about losing his hair, the contents of one of those bins caught his eye immediately. It was full to the brim with baseball-style caps. A bright red, with a shiny green dinosaur embroidered on the front. He could tell Laura about these caps when he saw her tomorrow. Better yet, he thought as his steps slowed and he reached into the bin to grab one of the caps, he could take it with him. It would save Laura a trip to a supermarket she probably didn't use and, right now, Tom was imagining the smile that might light up Harry's face if he liked the cap as much as Tom thought he would.

Carrying his bags into his apartment, he noticed the daughter of his elderly neighbour coming out of the door on the other side of the wide corridor.

'Carla! I haven't seen you for a long time. You've had Eileen staying with you since her hip surgery, haven't you? Is she back home now?'

'No.' The middle-aged woman shook her head. 'And it's not going to happen. We've had to move Mum into a retirement village with a good level of care available. I've been here for the last couple of days getting the apartment cleared out and ready.'

'You're going to sell?'

'Eventually. We want to rent it out for the moment, though, and see how that goes.' Carla smiled at Tom. 'You don't know of any nice, quiet, reliable people who are looking to rent a small apartment, do you? It's only got one bedroom but the sunroom can be a spare if it's needed. My kids used to sleep over when they were young. There's even a sandpit in the garden left over from those days, so it's perfect for grandparents.'

Or for a young, single mother, come to that. Tom blinked. This was getting to be a bit of a habit, having Laura popping into his head like this, but having to find a new place to live was one of the issues she was facing at the moment and passing on the information of something ideal being available was the sort of thing a friend should be only too happy to help with.

'I might know someone,' he said slowly. 'How much are you asking for rent?'

Carla named a figure that made him shake his head. 'Ah…that's a shame. I don't think that's within her budget.'

He turned to unlock his door. He could hear Carla locking up behind him and it suddenly sounded like a potential solution for Laura and Harry was being locked away. Not just any solution but one that was perfect at this time—a small apartment that wouldn't require so much time to look after so Laura would have more time to focus on Harry, and it was so close to the hospital for the many visits they were going to have to make. Or in case of any emergency. He would be next door, for that matter, in case of an emergency.

'Carla?'

'Yes?'

'I've got an idea.'

One that was rapidly gaining traction in his head. When Joe had told him about Laura's housing problem and the financial stress she was facing on top of everything else, he'd had to dismiss the idea of helping her because he knew how independent she was and that she could very well be offended by his offer. This time, however, it would be possible to keep it secret. For a while, anyway. Hopefully until this incredibly difficult patch of her life had been dealt with and after that…well, he didn't need to worry about that yet.

'It's a bit unusual,' he warned Carla, 'but you might be able to help me help someone else who really deserves a break. If you've got a minute, come in and I'll tell you all about her.'

'Is she a friend of yours?'

'We work together. She's a very impressive young woman and...'

Tom paused for a moment as he thought about how much he trusted Laura McKenzie and how today had proved that that trust was not misplaced. Of course something had changed between them by him stepping out of his comfort zone in order to offer her support. By holding her when she'd been so upset and by trusting her with his own personal story. But he still felt safe with her and he was confident that Laura felt safe with him, too.

'Yes,' he added firmly. 'She is a friend. And I know that she would be a perfect tenant. I just need to find out if she would be interested in living here.'

It wasn't far to go to find the paediatric oncology day unit in one of the Royal's wings when Tom had a break during his shift the next day. He had expected this area to be a very child-friendly space, with murals on the walls and bright colours everywhere. He hadn't expected to find Harry in a playroom surrounded by toys, games and other children, with his IV infusion on a pole that he could push around himself.

He also hadn't expected that Harry would recognise him. Or that he'd have a smile, albeit a bit shy, on his face even before he saw the gift that Tom had scrunched up in his hand. Laura was smiling too but her eyebrows were raised.

'What brings you here, Tom?'

'A few things,' he admitted. 'Firstly, I found something I thought Harry might like.' He shook the cap to restore its shape and then put it on his own head. 'It's a bit small for me, isn't it?'

Harry was grinning as he nodded.

'Do you think it might fit you?'

The nod became more enthusiastic so Tom put it on Harry's head. He tugged it into place and then looked up at his mother.

'It's gorgeous,' she said. 'And you know what? I think your teacher might let you wear it to school. How cool would that be?'

Tom couldn't help noticing that Laura's eyes looked shinier than normal when she caught his gaze over the top of Harry's head and mouthed, *Thank you.* He had to clear his throat. And then he shrugged so as not to make Harry's hair loss a big thing. Or to make too much out of the small gift.

'I also wanted to let you know that our intussusception case from yesterday is doing very well. It got caught before there was any major intestinal damage.'

'That's good to hear.' But Laura's attention was still on Harry, who had taken his cap off to look at the dinosaur embroidery and was now pulling it firmly back over what remained of his wispy hair. He walked off, pushing his IV trolley to where another small boy was watching a video on a television screen in the corner of the playroom.

'There was something else, too.'

'Oh?' Maybe Laura could hear the slightly tentative note in Tom's voice, because her eyes darkened a little.

'You remember my apartment block?'

'Um…yes?' Her gaze slid away from his instantly.

'What did you think of it? As a place to live, I mean?'

Laura was frowning now. 'I didn't take that much

notice, to be honest. But it seemed nice. And it's nice and handy for work for you. Why do you ask?'

'Because there's an apartment that's become available to rent and…and I know you're looking for somewhere smaller for you and Harry.'

Laura's breath came out in a huff of amusement.

'You're in a pretty exclusive part of town, Tom. I'd never be able to afford to live there.'

'You might be surprised. I think the rent is quite reasonable, actually.' Tom told her the amount he and Carla had agreed was believable and Laura's jaw dropped.

'No way…that's no more than I was paying for my room when we had four people living at my place.'

It was Tom's turn to avoid looking directly at Laura. 'Well…just between you and me, I know Carla would ask more from someone else. She's more interested in having a reliable and careful tenant and I told her that I might know just the person. A friend of mine that I'd be happy to recommend.'

Laura's mouth opened and then closed again. She was absorbing the word, wasn't she?

Friend. It had felt good to say it aloud but was he overstepping a boundary?

Apparently not.

'At that price I'd be very stupid not to be interested,' Laura said. 'It's perfect timing, too. With Harry only just starting his second cycle of chemo, we've got a bit of time up our sleeves to make a shift and get settled.'

'Here's Carla's card. She's the owner. The place is ready to go so she's keen to get a tenant in as soon as possible. She'll be delighted to hear from you.'

'Thanks…' She took the card. 'Maybe Harry and

I can go and have a look at it on our way home this afternoon.' She glanced over to where Harry was sitting on the floor. 'And thanks again for the cap. It was a brilliant idea and I know he loves it. He'll probably want to sleep in it for ever.'

'It looks as though Harry has been sleeping in that cap.'

'He has. It's his most treasured possession.' Laura unwrapped another mug from the sheet of newspaper and reached up to put it in the kitchen cupboard of her new apartment. 'Apart from his new sandpit, of course. As soon as he saw that, I knew I had to sign up for this place. He's got every one of his plastic dinosaurs out there already.'

'I saw him out there. It's nice to have the doors of the sunroom opening into the garden, isn't it?'

'It's a perfect bedroom for Harry.'

'You might want to check where we've put his bed.'

'You were so lucky to find this place.' Maggie pulled a potato masher from one of the stacked boxes. Baby Bella was asleep in her car seat beneath the kitchen table. 'What drawer does this go in?'

'The one under the cooktop. And it was Tom who found the apartment.'

'Good job, Tom.'

'It was hard to miss when I live right across the hall.' But Tom was enjoying the appreciation from both Laura and Maggie. Especially that smile from Laura. He hadn't her seen smile like that in a long time and the fact that he had made her life a bit happier made him feel very pleased with himself. He was enjoying a bit of a physical workout, as well, helping Joe shift the heavier pieces of furniture Laura was moving into her new apartment.

'Come on, Tom…' Joe was calling from the living room. 'You haven't earned your beer yet, mate. We need to empty this van. There's a couch calling.'

Mate…

It felt good to be part of this group, doing something that had nothing to do with work. Maybe he hadn't actually realised how isolated he'd made himself over the last few years. Or maybe this was just confirmation that he'd been right in thinking he'd finally dealt with his grief enough to be able to let people a bit closer. To step back into a life that would offer more than just work.

When Cooper and Fizz arrived with baby Harley, it felt like a party was happening.

'Sorry we couldn't get here early enough to help with the heavy stuff,' Cooper apologised. 'But some of us had to work.'

'You've brought the food.' Laura was beaming at the new arrivals. 'I can't believe we're having a taco night for our housewarming. It's been way too long.'

Tom eyed the cooler in Cooper's arms. 'Really? Like the tacos you had for your wedding breakfast?' The unconventional feast had been memorable. 'They were fantastic.'

'It became a flat tradition,' Laura explained. 'We got into the habit of taco nights once a week and anyone who wasn't on shift was welcome. You should have let us know you were a fan.'

Tom just smiled. Even a few months ago he would have shied away from being part of a group like this. It was Harry that had been the catalyst for change.

The jolt of feeling connected to a small boy who was potentially sick enough to be in danger had oddly not sucked him back into his past but pushed him forward into becoming more involved with people around him.

He hadn't expected that the change would have affected him so much but he was happier than he remembered being in a very long time. If he had to define the change, he'd say that he was feeling more alive with every passing week.

He'd needed people in his life. People that were more than simply work colleagues. He had walled himself off for so long, he'd clearly forgotten how important friends were.

Tom could still see through the open doors of the sunroom into the small, courtyard garden. An old tractor tyre had been used to create the sandpit in the corner of the garden and Harry had his dinosaurs lined up around the edge of it at the moment.

'You must have finished the second round of chemo by now,' he said to Laura.

'We have. And the AFP levels have fallen more than expected.'

'That's good news.' Alpha-fetoprotein levels were an important marker in monitoring treatment in liver cancer.

'It is. We've got another scan scheduled at the end of this week.'

'Oh, wow!' Fizz turned to join in the conversation. 'Does that mean that surgery could be close?'

Laura nodded. She was smiling but everyone could see that it was enough of an effort to look wobbly. It was such a double-edged sword, wasn't it? The surgery was the best hope for curing Harry completely but it wasn't something anyone wanted their child to have to go through.

'Oh, hon...' Maggie came out of the kitchen and wrapped her arms around her friend. 'It's going to be okay, you'll see.

'What's wrong with Mummy?' Nobody had seen Harry come inside and he was standing in the doorway, with two very sandy plastic toys in his hands.

'Oh...' Laura swiped under her eyes with her fingers. 'I'm just happy, sweetheart. We've got a lovely new house to live in and...guess what?'

'What?' Harry sounded suspicious. He edged closer to where Tom was standing.

'Cooper and Fizz have brought tacos for dinner. You love tacos, don't you?'

'Not tomatoes.' Harry took another step closer to Tom as if he was looking for some kind of protection. 'I hate tomatoes.'

'Me, too,' Tom said. 'Unless they're cooked. Raw tomatoes are kind of slimy.'

Harry looked up at him, tilting his head so far back his cap almost fell off, his mouth open with astonishment. His dark eyes looked huge, probably because they were such a focus in that small, pale face that had no hair to frame it now. But then the sides of his mouth curled up into a smile that made Tom's throat feel oddly tight.

It wasn't just a group of adult friends he'd been accepted into. This little boy thought he was okay, too, and that was enough to almost make Tom feel proud that he was not fond of raw tomatoes.

Laura was smiling, too. 'You're both excused tomatoes,' she said. 'But not lettuce, okay? Green food is important. Now, come on...' She beckoned Harry. 'Let's get those sandy hands washed.'

Over the next week or two, as Laura and Harry settled into their new home, Laura found that any worries she might have had about living as Tom Chapman's neighbour also settled. It wasn't as if she hadn't lived near workmates before. Maggie and Cooper had both been flatmates and, although they worked for the rescue base and not in the emergency department, she had seen them often enough in a professional setting. And Fizz had been a friend for a long time. It wasn't as if she and Tom were sharing a house, either—only a building—and it seemed as if they weren't even going to see that much of each other given that her hours were all over the place at the moment.

Laura glanced at his front door as she waited for Harry, who had gone back to find the library book he needed to return to school. It was nice knowing that Tom was there. Just across the hallway. That she had a friend nearby, if she needed one. It really did feel like a genuine friendship now. That emotional evening when they'd both shared things that were close to their hearts had opened a door into a space that was something to be treasured. A "friend" space, where it was perfectly safe to love people and care about what was happening in their lives. To help if it was ever needed.

Mind you, that help only seemed to be going in one direction currently. On top of everything else he had already done to help Laura, Tom had not only been directly responsible for solving both her housing and financial issues, he had pitched in and helped with the actual shifting process.

Although…now that Laura thought about it, that day had been the first time that Tom had been included into her wider group of friends in an informal social setting and that had to be a good thing for him, surely? He'd kept himself separate for as long as she'd known him and, while she could understand why he didn't want to let anyone too close, everybody needed friends, whether they realised it or not, so maybe she was helping him, as well. He had certainly seemed happy that day and had formed even more of a bond with Harry over their shared dislike of tomatoes.

'Harry? Hurry up, darling. I can't be late for work.'

He finally appeared, but without a book in his hand.

'Where's your library book? It needs to go back to school.'

'I don't want to go to school today.'

'Why not? Are you feeling sick?'

Harry didn't say anything but he shook his head. And then he reached up and pulled his hat off his head. A woollen beanie today, because someone at school had stolen his dinosaur cap yesterday. He'd cried himself to sleep and it had been hard work to convince him that another hat would be just as good. Now he was crying again.

'I hate this hat,' he sobbed. 'It's itchy…'

Laura looked down at his baldness and her heart broke. She stooped to gather her son into her arms. 'It's okay,' she told him. 'I'm going to ask Tom today where he got your cap and we'll go and find another one after school. It's just for one day. How 'bout I find your summer hat?'

But Harry shook his head again. He sat down by the front door, wrapped his arms around his legs and buried his face. Laura left his schoolbag beside him and sped back into the apartment to look for both the library book and a different hat.

She could hear voices as she came back and slowed down as she spotted Tom crouched down beside Harry. He was wearing a singlet and shorts and trainers and looked as though he'd just come back from an early-morning run. Having never seen him with so much bare skin, her steps faltered even more. This could be a little embarrassing for both of them. She could hear what Tom was saying now.

'Maybe it was because you were cool and some other boy wanted to look just like you.'

'But it was *my* hat.'

'It was. And whoever took it shouldn't have done that and I'm sorry it's made you unhappy, but you know what?'

Harry's intake of breath was a gulp. 'What?'

'I know where those hats come from. And I reckon there'll be another one there. You want me to see if I can find one?'

Laura couldn't hide out of sight any longer or she really would be late this morning. She couldn't pretend not to have heard what Tom was saying, either.

'There's no need to go to that trouble,' she said. 'If you tell us where to go, we can go after school. I'm finishing before three p.m. today so Harry doesn't need to go to afterschool care today.'

'It's no trouble.' Tom straightened and Laura was even more aware of all that bare skin. She focused on slotting Harry's library book into his schoolbag. 'It came from my supermarket and I'm going there today for groceries anyway. I'm on a day off.'

'I don't want to go to school.' Harry was crying again. 'Not without my special hat. My hat that Tom gave me...'

Laura caught Tom's gaze, trying to apologise for this early-morning inconvenience. But Tom didn't look bothered. He looked as though, like Laura, he was finding a small, bald and unhappy boy a heartbreaking sight.

'Tell you what, buddy. Let's make a deal.' He bent down again. 'You go to school with Mummy now. Mummy can tell me where your school is and when I've done my shopping I'll come to school and give you a new cap.'

Laura was shocked. 'You can't do that.'

'Why not?'

'It's your day off.'

'Which means I get to do exactly what I want.' Tom's gaze held hers a heartbeat longer and she got the message. He wanted to help. Who wouldn't want to help a sick child?

And that look on Harry's face as he looked up at Tom. Hero-worship, that's what it was. Tom was going right into his school, in front of all the other kids, like a knight in shining armour, and make Harry feel like the most special boy in the world. It would make them both feel good, she realised. All that she needed to do was shut down the uncomfortable feeling that she was letting Tom do far too much for them. For *her*. Maybe this was her problem, anyway, because it was so heart-warming to think that others cared and she couldn't afford to let herself start depending on that kind of support because it held the risk of undermining the independence she'd fought so hard to achieve.

Her hesitation made it impossible to protest any further. Harry was tugging at her hand.

'I want Tom to find me the new cap,' he said. 'He knows where the best ones are.' He scrubbed at his nose with his hand. 'Come on, Mummy…it's time to go to school.'

Standing outside the school gates as the bell rang at three-thirty p.m., Laura found she was thinking about Tom Chapman.

Again.

She'd been thinking about him on and off all day. Even though she knew he was having a day off, she'd found herself catching a glimpse of a tall, male figure in scrubs and feeling a beat of disappointment that it wasn't Tom. She'd been watching the clock, too, and wondering whether that precious replacement hat had been delivered in time for playtime. Or the lunch break. She'd warned the teacher that a strange man would be coming to find Harry at some point and, when she'd explained why, Harry's teacher had been delighted.

'Oh…what a lovely thing to do,' she'd said. *'We were all so upset when we couldn't find Harry's special cap yesterday.'*

She'd thought of Tom again when a young boy had come in with a broken arm from falling off his scooter. His mother was carrying a baby and that made her remember Tom and how gentle he'd been with baby Alfie. As it had then, thinking about him produced that lovely warmth that squeezed her heart and then trickled into the rest of her body.

Laura even wrapped her arms around herself, as if

to hold onto that warmth, as she watched for the junior school children to start pouring out of the doors as the bell rang, heading for the gates and their waiting parents. She'd be able to spot Harry instantly if he was wearing his new bright red and green dinosaur cap. She'd had a moment of real anxiety at work today, wondering if that supermarket might have run out of the caps. Would she still have a sad little boy to try and comfort this afternoon?

No…there he was, running out of the door the moment the bell rang. She could see the red cap even before he got out of the junior school building.

But then Laura could see another red cap. And another.

There was a surprised murmur running through the group of waiting parents. It seemed that every child coming out was wearing a red cap with a green dinosaur on the front. This wasn't a huge school but there had to be at least a hundred children in red caps filling the playground.

The first child to reach her mother was beaming. 'Look at my hat, Mummy.'

'Where did it come from?'

'A man came with a big box. We're all in Harry's club. We're allowed to wear our hats until he's feeling better and his hair grows back again.'

A man…

Laura was fighting back tears as she watched Harry coming towards her, with the proudest smile she had ever seen on his face. He was more than just special. He had a club of his own. Harry's club.

It wasn't just "a man" who'd dreamt this up. It was the nicest man in the world. That warmth that always came when Laura thought about Tom had just exploded into something that was totally overwhelming. He hadn't just totally won a small boy's heart for ever today. He had won a huge part of hers, as well.

She could feel it happening, singing in her veins and filling her heart so much it felt like it could explode.

Laura knew this feeling but recognising it was a shock.

Was she falling in love with Tom Chapman?

CHAPTER SIX

How had she not seen this coming?

The warning signs had been there all along, maybe from that very first connection Laura had felt with Tom which, ironically, had been that neither of them were interested in any kind of personal relationship. The safety net that had provided had been a breeding ground for the kind of trust that would never have been there otherwise.

And then Tom had become involved with Harry and he'd been there when Laura had been grappling with a parent's worst nightmare, facing a challenge that could mean she might lose her precious child. More than that, he understood what that was like because he'd been there himself and, unbelievably, he'd been prepared to risk his own health if it could save the life of a little boy that wasn't even his own.

She probably could have fallen in love with Tom at that moment if she hadn't been so overwhelmed by her own fears. She'd known something had changed between them but had wrapped it up in part of that safety net that made friendship perfectly acceptable and friendship with this particular, single man perfectly safe. Good grief...she had even convinced herself that living as his next-door neighbour wouldn't pose any kind of problems.

'Look, Mummy.' Harry held up a folded sheet of paper. On the outside there was a green shape that was obviously a T Rex and it now had colourful blobs surrounding it that had been covered with glue and then showered with a generous supply of glitter. 'Do you like my flowers?'

'They're gorgeous,' Laura said.

'Is Tom going to like my card?'

'He'll love it. Do you want me to help you with the writing to go inside?'

'No. I want to do it all by myself.'

'How 'bout I write the words on a different piece of paper and then you can copy them?'

'Mmm…' Harry looked up from under the brim of his new cap. ''Kay.'

'What do you want to say?'

'Thank you for my hat. I love you. From Harry.'

Laura swallowed hard. 'That's a lot of words. You could just say "Thank you from Harry" if you didn't want to do so much writing.'

Harry shook his head. 'Write it down, Mummy. What I said.'

Biting her lip, Laura wrote the words in big, clear letters on another piece of paper. She had to close her eyes for a moment after she wrote, 'I love you.' It wasn't the end of the world, was it? She loved her friends Maggie and Fizz and that was never going to be a problem. Maybe she just "loved" Tom and she wasn't actually in danger of being "in love" with him at all.

Harry used a pen and then did his best to copy the letters, working so slowly and carefully they wobbled enough to be only just legible. It was taking a long time, too. Enough time for Laura to let her mind put more effort into dealing with what was going on in her head. Or, possibly, her heart. Thoughts of Tom were never far away these days so it was easy to summon up a bit of a slideshow.

Like that look on his face when she'd told him about Harry's diagnosis. How gentle he'd been examining baby Alfie that day, with those long, clever fingers of his looking so big on such a tiny belly. The way he'd held her hand that night when he'd taken her to his home for coffee and how comforted she had felt being held in his arms. How disconcerted she'd been only this morning to see him in his running gear with all that skin exposed.

And…there it was.

She had some very clear images in her head now, of those surgeon's hands and those long, bare legs and arms—the skin dusted with dark hair and muscles outlined with a faint sheen of perspiration. The effect was that of a match was being scraped against sandpaper to light a tiny thrill of sensation as Laura's body and brain co-operated to make her wonder what it would be like to be touched by those hands. Or to run her own hands over the shape of those muscles. The pull of desire was so compelling, it actually stole her breath away.

This wasn't the kind of love that happened in a friendship. This was a magnetic pull that was far more powerful than any passing sexual attraction to someone because this had all the weight of a real re-lationship backing it up. The weight of trust. Of real kindness and caring. It wasn't that, as a single male, Tom had managed to slip past her barriers and into the space that her friends occupied in her heart. He was crashing into an even more private space. One that, until now, had only been occupied by Harry, as the most important person in her life.

And that was not acceptable, was it?

Not now, when Harry had to be the only thing that mattered.

Not ever, if she thought about how Tom would feel if he knew.

'I've finished, Mummy. Look…'

The prickle behind her eyes was pure pride that her little boy had put so much effort into this masterpiece with its spidery words inside.

'It's perfect, sweetheart. Let's get tidied up and then it's time for your bath.'

'But I want to go and give it to Tom.'

'I think he's still at work.' Laura had no idea where Tom actually was. She just knew she couldn't face him right now. What if he could see something in her face or feel the remnants of the kind of heat she had just created by thinking of him like that…?

Laura's heart was sinking fast. This new awareness had to be buried. Any twinge of physical attraction had to be stifled so thoroughly it wouldn't happen again, that's all there was to it. Compared to every other challenge Laura had going on in her life at the moment, surely this one should be completely manageable?

'Tell you what,' she said to Harry. 'We're going to be in the hospital tomorrow for your scan, remember? I can go and put it on his desk and then it'll be a lovely surprise.'

She could see that Harry was torn between wanting to hand over the card but knowing how much he liked surprises himself. The choice he made was a testament to how much of a hero Tom was to him now.

'You can put it on his desk. I think he likes surprises.'

The emergency department of the Royal was extremely busy when Laura took a few minutes away from Harry the next day to go to the ground floor area. The sedation Harry had needed in order to have the MRI scan had worn off but they had to wait for the results of the scan to be discussed and then Laura had an appointment with Suzie the surgeon and Hayley the paediatric oncologist.

Harry was very happy to have some time in the playroom in the paediatric ward, especially when he found that his friend Aroha was there. They curled up on some bean bags in front of the television screen and held hands as they watched a favourite movie, but Laura couldn't sit still with them. She was too nervous about the results she was going to hear about later. Had the chemotherapy shrunk the tumour? Were they going to schedule surgery or start another cycle?

'They're so cute, those two.' A nurse smiled at Laura. 'I'll be in here with them if you want to go for a walk. You look like you could use a distraction.'

So here she was, entering the ED and blinking a little at the controlled chaos she could see. It wasn't that unusual to see police officers or the hospital security guards in here but it advertised that there were potentially uncooperative or violent patients in the department and that was always enough to put Laura on edge. She could hear angry shouting coming from more than one of the cubicles.

On the plus side, with full cubicles and resuscitation areas and staff moving swiftly between too many patients, it was highly unlikely that she'd even be spotted going to Tom's office near the staffroom.

She could drop off Harry's card and be out of here in no time. The sooner the better, as far as she was concerned, because she wasn't quite ready to come face to face with Tom yet and test how difficult it was going to be to stifle how she felt about him now.

One of the junior doctors passed her in the corridor that led to the staffroom. 'You're not working today, are you, Laura?'

'No... I'm only here for two minutes to drop something off.'

'Just as well. It's crazy in here right now.'

'I can see that. What's going on?'

'There was a nasty fight in town between two gangs. We've got a lot of knife wounds and a few broken bones to sort out and some of them are as high as kites on meth or something. They're not exactly happy to be sharing the same ED, either, hence the reinforcements.'

Laura had already been nervous about what was going to be revealed in the meeting with Harry's doctors this afternoon and about whether things between herself and Tom Chapman were about to get awkward. Now she could throw in a dollop of anxiety that was a little too close to fear as the extent of the simmering violence in the department got a whole lot more real.

She took another few steps towards Tom's office but then she stopped dead in her tracks. What if Tom was in his office for some reason instead of out there in the department? Or what if he misinterpreted the thank-you message and thought that Laura might be using her son to get closer to Tom?

This was a bad idea. She could just tell Harry that Tom had loved his card—he didn't need to know that it hadn't actually been delivered, did he? Instead of going into Tom's office, Laura did an about-face. At the end of this corridor, she could turn left to go towards the reception desk in Emergency, right to go through the double doors that led to the main waiting area, or straight ahead to the doors that led into the rest of the hospital. Suddenly Laura couldn't wait to get back to the relative peace of the paediatric ward and to have a cuddle with Harry before she had to go to an appointment that had the potential to change her life again, for better or worse.

Without thinking, she walked purposefully straight ahead, only to find herself in the path of three leather-clad gang members who had obviously got past security in the waiting area and were storming in to find either their friends or their enemies in the treatment area. One of them swore viciously at Laura. Another one grabbed her arm.

'If you know what's good for you, you'll get out of our way, you stupid bitch...'

The grip of his hand on her arm was painful enough for Laura to know it would leave bruises but it was the tone of his voice and his words that made Laura freeze. Words that, if repeated often enough, became almost believable.

'You're so stupid...'
'It's your own fault, you ugly cow...'
'Just get out of my way...'

Words that took her back in time instantly. She was

about to be shaken. Or hurt. Or pushed down a set of stairs that would threaten both her own life and that of the baby she was carrying. Part of her knew perfectly well that this was only a flashback but it felt utterly real. Worse, even, because another part of her mind was telling her that these men could well be carrying knives or other weapons. She might be about to die and there was a silent scream in her head that was a name. A plea, perhaps.

Harry...

The huge man had both his hands on her now and Laura could feel the pure rage transferring itself into his grip and the force of the sideways shove that sent her flying, pushing against a stainless-steel trolley that crashed sideways with the sound of breaking glass. Through the blur of the noise and movement and her terror, she could sense action amongst the shouting around her and could see uniformed men converging on the group of intruders. It wasn't one of the policemen or security guards that broke her fall, however. It was one of the staff members in blue scrubs.

'Laura... Oh, my God, are you all right?'

It was Tom.

Tom, who was one of the people that Laura trusted the most in the world but right now he was gripping her arms to steady her balance and she hadn't yet processed the terror that the gang member had instilled.

'Let me go...' She could hear the panic in her own voice. 'Let me *go*...'

He let go instantly. Behind him, Laura could see that the gang members were being forcibly removed from the department but the damage had been done for Laura. She was shaking like a leaf. When her gaze raked Tom's face a heartbeat later, he was looking shocked enough for her to know that he was seeing far more than he should in her face.

Not what she'd been afraid he might see—that she'd thought she might be falling in love with him—but something much darker. Something she didn't want anybody to know about because she was so ashamed of that part of her past.

'I'm fine,' she told Tom. 'It was my fault—I wasn't looking where I was going.'

Oh, help…even her voice was weak and shaky. Laura pressed her hands to her forehead as she tried to take a deep breath. She hadn't actually been hurt in any way. She was overreacting and Tom wasn't the only person who was staring at her.

Somehow Laura gathered the strength she needed to lift her chin and raise her voice.

'I shouldn't even be in here.' She gave her head a sharp shake. She even managed a huff of something like laughter. 'I'm due in Paediatrics for an appointment with Harry's doctors. I've really got to go…'

She turned and took a step. And then another. From the corner of her eye she could see the way Tom was stretching out his hand as if he'd wanted to prevent her leaving just yet but nothing was going to stop her getting out of there.

It was all she could do not to start running, in fact.

He couldn't get it out of his head.

That look in Laura's eyes. That note of pure fear in her voice. She'd been afraid. He had felt that tension in her body as he had held her arms to make sure she had regained her balance. The very idea of her being so scared had been shocking. Yes, she'd just had a nasty fright by being abused by those gang members, but he had been the one holding onto her then and she had seemed just as terrified. Of *him*?

Tom couldn't understand it.

He'd known since he'd first met Laura that she had barriers up in her personal life and it had been a good thing for him because it meant that she was safe to work with. To be a friend, even, and it had been such a pleasure to be able to help her—and Harry. To finally able to be close enough to someone to feel connected and involved had added something to his life that he knew was important. Ever since Laura had brought Harry into the emergency department that day, Tom had known he was being pulled back into an engagement with life that was on a different—and more meaningful—level than the way he'd been living for the last few years.

It was bewildering to think that Laura could be afraid of him in any way.

Disturbing.

Unacceptable.

He needed to find out what was going on here. And to reassure Laura that she could trust him.

It was nearly nine o'clock that evening before Tom got home. He hadn't eaten but he wasn't hungry. He wouldn't be hungry, he decided, until he had found some answers to the questions that had been plaguing him since the incident in the department.

He knocked softly on Laura's door, not wanting to wake Harry if he was asleep. The moment she opened the door, his immediate thought was that Laura probably needed to be asleep herself. She looked so tired. Pale and…and far more vulnerable than Tom had ever seen her look. Maybe that was partly because her hair was hanging in soft waves to her shoulders instead of being tied up, the way it always was at work. Or perhaps it was because she was wearing an over-sized sweatshirt over her jeans and that made her look smaller. Younger.

Whatever it was, it triggered a powerful, protective instinct in Tom and all he wanted to do was to gather her into his arms and stroke her hair and tell her that everything was going to be okay. That he would make sure that everything was going to be okay.

But, of course, he didn't do that. He cleared his throat instead.

'I just wanted to check that you were okay,' he said.

Laura nodded.

'And Harry's okay?'

She nodded again.

'You said that you had a meeting with his doctors this afternoon?'

'Yes.' He could see the muscles in Laura's throat moving as she swallowed hard. 'It was good news. The tumour's shrunk a lot. They're confident that it can be completely resected with surgery.'

Tom took a beat to process that news. It was the best news to have this soon—after only two cycles of chemotherapy. It also meant that Harry would be facing major surgery, probably very soon, however, and that had to be terrifying for Laura.

'How soon?' he asked quietly. 'For the surgery?'

'Next week.' Laura pressed her fingers against her

lips as if she wanted to stop them trembling. Or to stop herself bursting into tears.

'It's good news.' Tom found a gentle smile to try and reassure her. 'He's going to get through this.'

Laura nodded again. 'I know… He's not even scared. He's excited by the idea of spending time in hospital because his friend Aroha is having her heart surgery next week, too. They'll be in the ward at the same time.'

'And you? How are you doing?'

'I'm okay.' Her smile was unconvincing. 'It's nice of you to ask.'

'I was worried about you after what happened in ED today.' He tried to hold Laura's gaze, willing her not to look away from him.

She didn't look away but she wasn't saying anything out loud. What was it he could see in her eyes? It felt like some sort of apology, but why?

'You know you can trust me, don't you, Laura?'

Another nod. She still wasn't breaking the eye contact. There was more than an apology to be seen. Now it felt like she was searching for something. And it felt as though he was the only person that might be able to give it to her.

'I know there's something going on that you're not talking about,' he said gently. 'So, talk to me…please. I can't go away until you do because I'm not going to stop worrying.'

The silence was even longer this time, but then Laura stepped back, pulling the door open a little further. 'You'd better come in,' she said.

He'd told her about his past, hadn't he? He'd shared something that she was pretty sure he'd never shared with anyone else so he deserved the same level of trust. Laura knew he'd been shocked this afternoon, as well. That he had seen her fear. She remembered how instantly he'd taken his hands off her body and it occurred to her now that he might have thought she was afraid of him as well as those gang members. He deserved to know that that was the opposite of the truth. That he was probably the person she trusted more than anyone else on earth.

As a bonus, if she needed a test to see if her feelings could be stifled, then here it was. And after the emotional exhaustion of the tension of waiting to hear about Harry's scan and the huge fright she'd got when she'd been pushed around in ED, how she felt about Tom Chapman was only a background buzz. Laura couldn't decide whether that made it rather nice to have him here or whether it was going to be the final straw in a tough day.

'I think I need a glass of wine,' she said, as Tom followed her back into her small living room. 'It's been quite a day.'

'Let me.' Tom took the bottle from her hands and then the corkscrew. 'I'd love one myself. Is Harry asleep?'

Laura took a peek into the sunroom and then quietly shut the door so they wouldn't disturb him. 'Out like a light. It was a big day for him, too. Plus he's still got some sedatives in his bloodstream, I expect.'

She took the glass from Tom and he followed her example to head for the couch. For several minutes, they sat sipping their wine in what started as a companionable silence but then it became loaded. Without even catching his gaze, Laura knew that Tom was waiting for her to say something.

'I guess I kind of overreacted today, didn't I?'

'When you said that what happened was your fault? Yeah…' Tom turned his head and she was forced to meet his gaze. 'I wouldn't say overreacted, exactly. It seemed to me more like a reaction that you might have been forced to have.'

His dark eyes were full of concern. A hint of anger, even?

'It wasn't your fault, Laura. Not in any way, shape or form. You had every right to be there. And, even if you didn't, the only person at fault was the lowlife who assaulted you.'

'Mmm…' Laura took a large swallow of her wine. 'I know that… It's just…'

She could feel Tom's gaze still on her. 'It's just that you've been hurt before, isn't it?'

Laura bit her lip. She didn't want to admit it.

'Was it Harry's father?'

A sideways glance reassured her that Harry was blissfully unaware of anything that was being said out here. 'He wasn't like that to begin with. He was really charming. Easy to fall in love with. But he started drinking more and more and then his mates got him into drugs.'

It sounded like Tom was speaking with a clenched jaw. 'How bad was it?'

'He just got angry a lot at first. Shouted at me. Said a lot of nasty stuff. He made it seem like it was my fault. I was still in love with him so it was easy to be made to feel… I don't know…worthless, I guess. I tried to change. To make it better…'

Tom made a sound like a soft growl. 'As if you would ever need to change, Laura. You're super-smart. Kind. The best mum and…well, look at you. You're gorgeous.'

The praise was more than comforting. Did Tom really believe that? And, if he did, was there actually a possibility that they could end up being closer than just friends? Laura didn't look up to meet his gaze but she was looking at his hands and she could feel the tingle of strong emotions that were gathering force.

Sheer longing. To be touched. Not sexually, necessarily—just the contact. She desperately wanted the reassurance that touch could be trusted. That it was safe to love someone, perhaps.

'I only stayed with him as long as I did because he promised to get clean. After I found out I was pregnant. He said he couldn't do it without my help and I think he really tried, too…but…'

'But?'

'He got high. When I was six months pregnant. He got angry. I…ah…fell down some stairs. That was why Harry was so premature.'

Tom was silent for a long moment. 'You said he was dead when we were talking about finding a donor for Harry if it was needed. Was that true?'

'Yes. He died of an overdose—not long after I'd told him it was over. He was drinking again, just before Harry was due to come home from the hospital, and I told him I was going to do whatever it took to keep my baby safe from him.'

'And you did.' Tom touched her arm, just letting his hand settle there for a heartbeat, warm and heavy and solid. 'You still are—doing everything to keep your son as safe as possible.'

The physical touch was more a congratulatory gesture than anything else. It shouldn't have made that longing kick up so many notches that it was almost painful. Laura drained the last of the wine in her glass.

'Can I get you another one?'

She shook her head. 'I'd probably fall over. I'm so tired.'

'I'm not surprised.' Tom got to his feet. 'I should go, too.'

Laura stood up, as well. It had to be more the exhaustion and stress of the day that made her wobble slightly because one glass of wine would never do that. It wasn't even that much of a wobble but it was enough for Tom to notice. For him to turn and put his hand on her arm again.

They were so close. Laura could see the thick tangle of Tom's eyelashes, how dark his eyes were, and the concerned frown line between those eyes. For a moment she was transported back to that time in his office when she'd felt as if he understood her fear for her child better than anybody else could. Now it felt as if he understood exactly why she had reacted the way she had to the violent situation in the emergency department today. And that he didn't think she was stupid. Or ugly. Or any of the things that had once undermined her self-esteem so badly. It also looked as though he'd meant every one of those nice things he'd said about her.

'It was never your fault,' Tom said quietly. 'Not back

then and not today. You do realise that you deserve so much more than feeling like that, don't you?'

Laura couldn't say anything. She could feel the warmth of Tom's breath on her face and she was fighting the urge to lean closer to his body. Like the touch he'd given her on her arm moments ago, Tom leaned down and gave her a one-armed hug, made slightly awkward by the wineglass he had in his other hand. Laura responded but tilted her head to check where her own wine glass was and somehow her face brushed his.

Or rather her lips brushed his.

Just for a nanosecond, she froze in shock, because that touch was so electric she could feel it throughout her entire body. Almost as fast, however, her head jerked back.

'Oops... Sorry... That wasn't meant to happen.'

Tom was straightening slowly. 'It was my fault, I think. Clumsy.'

Laura shrugged. She found a huff of laughter, even. 'It's like when you try to move aside for someone in the street and they move the same way and you do that awkward little dance.' She took the wineglass from Tom's hand. 'Let me take that. Thanks for popping in to check up on us.'

Us. Because he'd asked about Harry, too. Because they were neighbours. Friends.

She just needed her entire body to shut down that ache. The one that was telling her how much more she wanted from Tom right now. Something that she was never going to get, judging by the way he was avoiding looking directly at her now. He picked up the laptop bag he'd put down when he'd come in.

'You sure you're okay?'

Laura's nod was brisk. 'Just tired.' She needed to be alone. She suspected she might want to have another glass of wine. Or cry. Or to think about that almost, accidental kiss. Probably all of the above. 'Goodnight, Tom.'

CHAPTER SEVEN

WELL…WHO WOULD have thought a single glass of wine could have that much of an effect?

Tom Chapman shut his front door behind him and then leant against it, his hand against his forehead, middle finger and thumb massaging his temples.

Even after a couple of deep breaths, he could still feel it, though.

That…tingle. The first real signs of life in that particular part of his anatomy since he'd been hurled into that world of grief and loss. And, yeah…maybe he'd been aware that it wasn't normal not to have sexual awareness or needs for this long but he'd never bothered seeking any advice or therapy.

Life was easier this way. Like it was to not tell people about his past.

Or it had been, anyway. Until he'd had an ill-advised glass of wine on a completely empty stomach after a somewhat challenging day. Until that moment when Laura had turned her head in an unexpected direction and their lips had brushed each other's. Awakening of any kind of physical needs was not only a bit of a shock, it had been utterly inappropriate, given what

Laura had just been telling him about her previous relationship with Harry's father.

Okay...this was better. Tom pushed himself off the wall. He was feeling slightly sick now and he couldn't blame that on a single glass of wine. It was the thought of Laura having been in an abusive relationship that was turning his stomach and there was a central core of anger there, as well. How could anyone have treated her like that? To hurt her... Not just physically, although the implied violence of her having been pushed down some stairs that had ended with Harry's premature birth made that knot of anger white hot. No...it was the more insidious damage that had been done to Laura's self-esteem that was disgusting him.

Any decent human being would be so horrified by that they would want to offer sympathy and reassurance but Tom hadn't just been saying whatever he thought might help. He had believed everything he had said to Laura, especially that she deserved so much more than that. She was an extraordinarily intelligent woman and such a caring mum.

As he put a frozen meal into his microwave and hit the buttons to get his overly late dinner on the way, Tom found himself remembering that day she'd brought Harry into the emergency department. That moment when he'd reached the gap in the curtains around that cubicle and had seen her almost on the bed with Harry, her arm around him and that look of pure love on her face as she smoothed back his hair. He could even feel an echo of that punch in the gut it had given him. The flashback to knowing what it was like to feel that kind of love for your child—and for your partner. To be...a *family*...

It still felt like longing. Hunger, even.

Of course it does, you idiot... Tom shook his head as the microwave pinged and he took out the plastic container. He hadn't eaten since breakfast and his blood sugar had to be rock bottom. It was no wonder his body was given off strange signals.

He needed food. And sleep.

Tomorrow was another day and Tom happened to know that Laura was not rostered on to work.

Which was a good thing, he decided as he took his first mouthful of a sadly unappetising meal. He needed to push a reset button of some kind in his life that would take him back to where things felt normal. And safe. To a time when Laura McKenzie and her son did not occupy this disconcerting amount of space in his head.

Or his heart, for that matter. Like always, when you decided not to think about something so much, it popped into your head with renewed strength and this time, it was that shocking memory of how frightened Laura had looked when he'd caught her arm after she'd been pushed by that thug. And it definitely wasn't his head that was generating such a powerful urge to offer his protection. That could only have come from his heart.

Tom took a moment, during the next afternoon, to congratulate himself on a plan that was definitely coming together. It had been a busy morning in the Royal's emergency department and he hadn't been distracted in any way from doing the best job he could. Life felt perfectly normal.

One case in particular, a challenging multi-trauma

from a car that had rolled as it left the road and then wrapped itself around a tree, had kept him and the rest of the resus team flat out for well over an hour as they'd stabilised the young man enough to get him to Theatre.

'It was touch and go, that surgery,' Fizz told Tom when he found her snatching a break in the staffroom. 'He went into cardiac arrest twice.'

'Doesn't surprise me. I was amazed that we got him to Theatre. He must have lost his entire blood volume with that pelvic fracture slicing his artery.'

'He was in Theatre for hours but it sounds like he's stable now. He'll be in Intensive Care for a while, though.'

'I might go and visit later. I'd like to have a chat to the surgeon and see what he found. I'm sure some of that blood loss was coming from other internal injuries but it was hard to tell on the ultrasound. Do you know if they took out his spleen? Or had to repair a liver laceration?'

Fizz shook her head. 'Speaking of livers, did you know that Harry's got his surgery date now? For next week?'

'Oh?' Tom busied himself making peeling off the plastic from a packet of vending machine sandwiches. He didn't want to admit that he'd been talking to Laura late last evening. Part of today's plan was to try not to even think about it.

'Wednesday.' Fizz nodded. 'I was talking to her last night.'

Tom raised an eyebrow. Had that been before or after his visit? he wondered. And what had the good friends discussed? Maybe Laura had told Fizz that Tom had almost kissed her?

Dammit…that was the one thing he was really trying not to think about and now it was too late. Even as he pushed the thought from his head, he could feel that damned tingle again. At least Fizz didn't seem to think anything was out of the ordinary so maybe Laura hadn't said anything.

'I had a chat to Maggie, too,' Fizz continued. 'We're going to try and arrange things so that one of us can be with her the whole time that Harry's in Theatre. A liver resection can take quite a few hours sometimes.'

'It's a major operation, all right.'

'They're taking his gall bladder out, as well, because the tumour's on the right side of the liver. But they're only taking one section, which is good. It'll probably only take a few weeks to regenerate completely.'

Tom was listening but his attention wasn't a hundred percent. He could still feel the echoes of that tingle. Maybe it was only natural that his body was waking up again after so long. It didn't mean he was going to lose control and end up back in the kind of space that made it possible to fall in love with someone and start making plans for a future together. No…all it meant was that he might need to allow the physical release of sex back into his life and it would be easy enough to do something about that. It wasn't as if he'd ever been short of opportunities.

Like Hannah, there… He returned the smile of the young registrar who had just come into the staffroom. Blonde, blue-eyed and—as far as he knew—single, she had given him the impression for quite a while that she might welcome a chance to spend some time together away from work. He'd need to be careful, of course, and make sure that he was very clear right from the start that he wasn't looking for anything serious or long term.

But…

But Tom realised that that tingle had faded completely in the short space of time that he'd been considering that option. Perhaps it was simply because he'd never been open to the idea of casual sex with colleagues, not even before he'd met and fallen in love with Jenny. He had long ago accepted that he would never have another relationship like that. Did this mean he might have to accept living like a monk for the rest of his life?

'So…do you want to be on the roster?'

'Sorry?' Tom looked up as Fizz pushed her chair back and stood up.

'I heard about the dinosaur caps.' Fizz was smiling at Tom. 'That was such a cool thing to do and it's no wonder Harry thinks you're a super-hero. I thought you might like to be on the roster we're making so that we can make sure that Laura's got all the support she needs while Harry's in hospital and then recuperating at home.'

Tom had a new image in his head now—that smile on Harry's face when he'd turned up at his school with the carton of supermarket baseball caps. Now, that had been special. He could feel the same squeeze in his chest again just remembering it. A mix of something very warm and poignant enough to give him a bit of a lump in his throat but it wasn't a pull back into heart-wrenching territory. It was a positive thing—part of the new involvement with life that might be throwing up some left-field challenges but Tom knew it was healthy. He just needed to give himself time to adjust.

'I'll do whatever I can to help,' he told Fizz. 'You can count on that.'

It was the longest day of Laura's life.

They had warned her how long Harry's surgery might take but what she hadn't been prepared for was that time seemed to slow down so that every minute felt more like an hour and the hours were interminable.

Even after Harry came out of Theatre, it was another couple of hours before he was settled into his bed in the paediatric intensive care unit and the medical team was happy that every monitoring device was functioning perfectly and that the recordings being made were not raising any concerns.

It was only then that Laura could take a breath and shift into the next phase of this ordeal—the one where she sat beside Harry's bed and kept watch over her precious son. Following every rise and fall of that small chest for the longest time but then letting her gaze rest on his face, searching for any sign that he might be in pain despite the sedation. Becoming attuned to the soft beeps of various monitors, she could be alert for any change in their patterns of sound at the same time.

Harry's nurse came in at very regular intervals to take note of his heart rate and blood pressure and oxygen saturation levels, to check drainage tubes for any sign of haemorrhage and to record fluid input and output. So many things to keep an eye on but she took note, also, of how Laura was coping.

'When did you last have something to eat?'

'I'm really not hungry.'

'Come into the staffroom and have a cup of tea and a biscuit, at least.'

'I'm drinking water. I'm fine.' If anything, Laura edged closer to Harry's bed. 'I can't leave him. Even going to the loo stresses me out. What if he woke up and I wasn't here?'

'That's not going to happen. He's well sedated and I'm checking on him often enough to see any signs of that lifting. We've got his pain management well under control at the moment' Her face creased with concern. 'You need to rest, too, Laura. You know what we always tell the parents—that you've got to look after yourself if you want to be able to do a good job looking after your child.'

'Yeah, yeah... I know. I'll rest, I promise. I've slept in a chair before.'

That had been back in the days when Harry had been in his incubator in the neonatal ICU, mind you—such a tiny baby who shouldn't have needed to struggle because of an untimely entrance to the world. It felt like a lifetime ago but the feeling of being sucked into an occasional doze, giving her brain a brief respite from the exhausting anxiety, was very familiar.

It was in those moments as she slipped towards unconsciousness that Laura remembered—and felt very grateful for—the support her friends had given her throughout this longest ever day. How blessed was she to have so many good friends? Fizz had brought coffee and doughnuts to the waiting area before she'd started work today and Maggie had stayed for hours, with baby Bella snuggled into her sling, being the most perfect baby in the world. Cooper had come in that afternoon, with little Harley, who'd played with the toys in the corner, and Joe had managed to sneak a few minutes to come and visit after delivering a patient to the emergency department.

It had been Tom who had been the last visitor to come and keep her company in that small waiting room and…and it had been fine. There hadn't been the slightest awkwardness left over from the last time they had been alone together when that accidental, almost kiss had happened, despite how often it had replayed itself in Laura's mind since then. Right now, it might never have happened as far as any effect it was having.

It had actually felt astonishingly appropriate that it was Tom who was with her when the surgeon himself came to tell her that it was all over and that the surgery had gone as well as they could have hoped for. It was, after all, Tom who'd been there when the shocking diagnosis had been made in the first place—who'd been responsible, in fact, for it being picked up as early as it had been.

What if someone else had missed feeling that abnormality in that child-sized liver and the cancer had had a whole lot more time to spread? That was something else to be grateful for. Not only that, it was Tom who'd put up his hand to be a potential living donor and that had felt almost like an insurance policy at a time when Laura had been feeling so helpless in not being able to provide that gift herself if it ever became Harry's only hope of a cure.

And…of all people, it was Tom who could really understand the emotion of that moment when she'd heard that the surgery was over and had, apparently, been successful. The connection Laura felt to Tom had never been as strong as it was in that moment.

The depth of her love for him was just as profound but there was no fear at all of him reading too much in her face because that intense connection and the emotion that went with it was simply a background to the only thing that mattered here, to both of them.

Harry.

Tom had stayed with her during that tense time of transferring Harry from Recovery to the paediatric ICU and Laura was enormously grateful for that. She was grateful to all her friends for their support today, of course, but it was Tom whom she was thinking about most often as exhaustion pulled her towards sleep.

And then her head would drop and she would jerk into wakefulness again. It always felt as if she'd had a fright so she would have to start checking everything all over again. Listening carefully to the steady beeping of all the monitors. Watching Harry breathe. Touching his cheek or his hand with a gentle finger to check that he wasn't too hot or too cold. Trying to analyse any perceived flutter of his eyelids or twitch of his lips.

By the next morning, Laura had that spaced-out sensation that came from a total lack of sleep and she was more easily persuaded to take a short break in the relatives' room just outside the intensive care unit, when Fizz arrived with hot coffee and breakfast muffins. Due to the risk of infection, visitors to Harry's bedside were very restricted.

'Tom called us all last night to let us know how Harry was doing. He sounded very positive.'

'It's looking good so far.' Laura managed a few bites of the bacon and egg muffin but it was the coffee she really needed. 'They're going to keep him in the unit for another twenty-four hours or so—mainly to make sure his renal function is good and that pain management is adequate.'

'I'll let Maggie know that she'll need to text when she comes in today. I think she's planning to bring you some lunch but I'll make sure she knows you won't want to be away from Harry for too long.'

'Thanks, Fizz.' Laura hugged her friend. 'I'd better get back now, actually. I know he's far too sleepy to really notice whether I'm there or not but it makes me feel better.'

'Of course it does. Make sure you get some sleep sometime, though. I bet you didn't get much last night.'

Fizz wasn't the only person to be concerned about Laura's lack of any real rest. By early that evening, it was the consultant in charge of ICU who was trying to persuade her to get a few hours of sleep.

'I'd give you one of the on-call rooms here but we've got extra staff on at the moment and they're all reserved, I'm sorry.'

'It's fine, honestly. I'll be able to sleep in the chair tonight. I was just too stressed last night.'

'But you live pretty close to the Royal, don't you?'

'Yes, she does.'

Laura's head swung to see Tom coming through the door of Harry's room. 'Five minutes' walk away, in fact. A two-minute run. Is there any reason she needs to stay close at the moment?'

'No.' The consultant was smiling. 'We're delighted with Harry's progress and we're going to lighten his sedation and look at transferring him to the ward but we won't be doing that before tomorrow morning.

Which leaves plenty of time for Laura to get a bit of proper sleep. We'll let you know if there's the slightest change.'

Tom's smile was persuasive. 'Think about it, Laura. Home for a hot shower and some clean clothes. A few hours in your own bed.'

'I…can't…'

'You want to be on top of your game in the morning, don't you? When Harry wakes up?'

'Of course I do…but…what if I fall asleep and don't hear my phone if they text or call me?'

'Okay…' Tom nodded, as if the matter was settled. 'That's no problem. I'll leave my number as well and they can call me. I'll be right next door and I promise that I'll hear my phone if you don't. Consider me an insurance policy.'

That penetrated the fog in Laura's brain. She'd used that phrase herself, thinking about Tom, hadn't she? She knew she could trust him and, given the vague confusion that was always part of total physical and emotional exhaustion like this, it was actually very comforting to have someone else taking charge like this. Rather like that night when she'd been sitting on the hospital steps, so upset, and he'd taken hold of her hand to lead her somewhere more private.

'You'll be there, Tom?' she checked.

'I'll walk home with you. I'll bring you back first thing in the morning or whenever you feel you have to be back here, as long as you've had a good few hours' sleep. I'll be just across the hallway. You'll only have to knock on my door.'

Laura let her gaze soak in the peaceful expression on Harry's face as he lay there, deeply asleep. She listened to that steady beat of the monitors and then caught the gaze of Harry's nurse.

'I'll be here,' the nurse promised. 'We'll have some-one with him the whole time, I promise. Please, Laura. You need to rest before you fall over or get sick. Harry needs you to look after yourself.'

Her feet felt wooden as she walked out of the unit—as if she really could fall over far too easily. But she didn't have to stop moving because she had Tom walk-ing by her side and, if she did fall over, he would be there to pick her up. It was amazing how a human safety net like that could give you so much more strength, wasn't it?

It felt as if she could cope with anything as long as she had Tom Chapman walking beside her.

'I don't think I can cope with this.'

Tom closed the door of Laura's apartment behind him, having followed her inside to make sure she was okay. Clearly, she wasn't, because she had walked into the living area and was now frozen in one spot, star-ing at the door to the sunroom that was Harry's bed-room. When she turned her head, Tom could see how overwhelmed she was. There were tears gathering in her eyes and her voice was trembling.

'It feels too empty,' she added in little more than a whisper. 'I don't want to be here on my own...with-out Harry.'

'No problem.' It felt good to recognise a problem and be able to solve it so easily. 'I'll stay here with you. I can sleep on the couch.'

'I can't ask you to do that.'

'You're not asking, I'm offering.' Tom could sense

that Laura was relieved, as she had appeared to be when he'd taken charge at the hospital and persuaded her to come home for a break. 'You have a shower and I'll find something for us to eat.'

'I don't think I've got much in the fridge.'

'That's not a problem, either. I've got a freezer full of microwave dinners. You have the choice of lasagne, spaghetti bolognaise or possibly a fish pie.'

If nothing else, he'd succeeded in distracting Laura for a moment. 'Microwave dinners?' There was even a hint of a smile on her face. 'When this is all over, Tom, I might have to teach you how to cook. Spaghetti bolognaise is one of Harry's favourites so it's become one of my specialties.'

'It's a deal. Okay… I've got my phone in my hand, see? I'll be back in five minutes and I expect to hear that shower running.'

He could, indeed, hear the shower running when he returned with the frozen, boxed meals in his hands. Because Laura hadn't made a choice, he'd brought the whole selection and he put them in the oven to heat up, rather than the microwave, so that he could do them all at the same time. It would take nearly an hour but… yes… Laura had half a bottle of white wine in her fridge. A glass or two of that and she'd be out like a light as soon as her head hit the pillow.

The image of Laura with a wine glass in her hand generated another one of those disturbing tingles because it reminded him of the last time he'd been in this apartment with her but it was stronger this time, probably because Tom was aware of the sound of the shower running in the bathroom of this small apartment.

Okay…make that rather too aware that Laura was

standing beneath that water, totally naked. Possibly with soap bubbles cascading over her skin as she shampooed her hair... Tom had to close his eyes as he fought off that image. What was going to happen later, he wondered, when he was lying on that couch in her living room, aware of her in her bed, on the other side of a thin wall? At least she wouldn't have to worry about him not hearing a phone call, he decided. It was very likely going to be his turn tonight to not get a very restful sleep.

Laura emerged from the bathroom with her hair hanging in damp curls over a rust-coloured sweatshirt and her long legs encased in black leggings. Her feet were bare and her face free of any makeup and she looked nothing like Tom had ever seen her look, either at work or in civvies. Was that why he was suddenly aware of so many details of how she looked? Even with her hair damp, the overhead light was picking out the auburn tints, making it come alive as if it was full of tiny flames. Warm brown eyes were the perfect colour with those autumn-coloured waves and Tom could see the smattering of soft freckles dusting her pale skin.

He'd told her she was gorgeous, that night he'd been trying to reassure her that she deserved something so much better than she'd had with Harry's father. He had been telling the truth, that was for sure. Laura McKenzie had to be one of the most beautiful women he'd ever seen. Especially when she smiled like that...

'That feels so much better.'

'Can you stay awake long enough to eat something? It's going to take a while to heat up.'

'I could use the time to pack some things that Harry's going to need when he's feeling a bit better. Like some books and toys and videos.'

Tom could see her hesitating in front of the door to Harry's room so he walked towards her. 'Need some help?'

'Sure…'

When she moved again, Tom was close enough to feel the brush of air on his skin from her movement. He thought he could feel the warmth of Laura's freshly clean skin, even. He could definitely smell the scent of her shampoo or soap or whatever it was that was flowery and fresh at the same time, like how he imagined the blossoms of a lemon tree might smell.

'Oh…some of his dinosaurs are out in the sand-pit.' Laura suddenly turned. 'I mustn't forget them…'

She hadn't stopped her forward momentum as she turned and Tom hadn't stopped his, either, so it became one of those clumsy moments of accidental body contact, like that awkward, one-armed hug had been when they'd both been holding wine glasses. Their lips had been the point of the accidental contact that time but this time it was their bodies, with Laura's breasts brushing against his arm. Even more startling than the unexpected touch, however, was the flare of something he could see in Laura's eyes. It looked a lot like…

…like something he was feeling himself but he didn't know quite what it was.

A connection that was too powerful to ignore?

A need for physical contact that was born from a very particular kind of loneliness?

Just plain, simple desire?

Whatever it was, they were both feeling it. That had to be what made them both move at the same time, turning towards each other rather than away and, a heartbeat later, to be touching lips in a kiss that was the absolute opposite of accidental. It was also totally different from any kiss Tom could ever remember having and it was so utterly astonishing he knew it was going to be very difficult to stop.

But that was exactly what he had to do. Laura was not only his friend, she was exhausted and very vulnerable right now. However powerful this wave of physical need was suddenly becoming, what kind of man would take advantage of a vulnerable woman?

'Noo...' Laura's tiny groan echoed one that Tom hadn't uttered as he eased the pressure of his lips on hers. He still hadn't opened his eyes when he felt her wrap her arms more tightly around his neck.

'Don't stop...' Her whisper came from lips so close to his own, he could feel her breath as if it was his own. 'I need this, Tom... I need it *so* much...'

He heard the way she swallowed—as if it was painful. 'Just this once,' she said, so quietly it might have been in his imagination. Something that he was thinking of saying himself? 'Just tonight...'

How could he pull away now?

Yes, Laura was vulnerable right now. And exhausted. She needed comfort. A break from the unbearable tension she'd been under for so many weeks, let alone the exacerbation of that in the last two days. If he could provide distraction and comfort in the form of a physical release, was it so terrible that he wanted it so much himself?

Whatever argument was going on in his head was rapidly getting muffled as he kissed Laura again and, this time, the intensity of the kiss spiralled into a headlong dive into sheer passion. When he dropped his hands from her back to her hips and then slid them upwards again over the silky smooth skin beneath her sweatshirt, to find that she hadn't bothered putting a bra back on after her shower and Laura pressed herself into his hands with a tiny moan of need, Tom knew he was lost. That he needed this as much as Laura did. That this was exactly how powerful this needed to be in order for him to break through a barrier he'd believed was there for the rest of his life.

Oh... Dear Lord...

He was being so gentle with her that it made Laura want to cry but, at the same time, she could feel the strength behind that touch. Those kisses…and it made her feel safe.

Loved, even.

This was about so much more than just sex. It was about more than about a release of unbearable tension that had been building ever since she'd learned how sick Harry was. This felt like an acknowledgment of the connection she had found with Tom. About feeling understood. Worthwhile. It didn't matter that it was just this once because this was exactly what Laura needed right now and she shut off any thoughts about anything else and just let herself sink into the sheer deliciousness of physical sensation.

Pleasure that built and built until it exploded into wave after wave of ecstasy. Somehow it wasn't surprising to find that her cheeks were wet with tears as she tried to catch her breath but they became a release all of their own when they wouldn't stop easily.

'It's okay…' Tom used the sheet he'd pulled over

them both to mop up her tears and then he pulled her more closely into his arms. 'It's okay...'

And it was. Because she was lying here in his arms and she could feel the steady thump of his heartbeat beneath her cheek. She could also feel the blessed reprieve of a deep sleep just a breath or two away. Tom was saying something about food that would be ready to eat but Laura could only murmur her total lack of interest. She wasn't hungry.

She had everything she could possibly need for now.

CHAPTER EIGHT

'YOU SHOULD WRITE this up for a paramedic journal, Tom.' Joe was shaking his head as he studied the ECG graph on the table in front of him. 'Just look at that massive ST elevation. Most people would assume that this guy was having a cardiac event.'

'ECG changes from traumatic brain injury are pretty well documented now,' Tom responded. 'But it is a dramatic difference when you look at how normal the ECG is once we intubated him. Why don't you write it up? Never hurts to have a few publications on your CV.'

'For when I go hunting for a new job, you mean?' Joe grinned at his crew partner for the day. 'I'm quite happy where I am, thanks, mate.'

Tom smiled back. 'Me, too.'

In fact, he realised that he hadn't felt this happy in... well, he couldn't actually remember how long it had been. He did know that, at least in part, some of this new contentment with life had something to do with that night he'd spent with Laura.

Not immediately, mind you. The early hours of the morning after had had its moments of uncomfortable awkwardness when he was sure they were both thinking they might have made a terrible mistake. Then they'd walked back to the hospital together and agreed that it had been special—a kind of gift, even—but it had been simply a one-off extension of their friendship that nobody else needed to know about. Laura had been the one who'd broached the subject.

'It was the last thing I expected to happen but exactly what I needed,' she'd said. 'A total distraction and the ultimate physical comfort, but I know it was above and beyond the call of being a friend. Don't worry… It won't happen again…'

Being that close had brought them closer together, of course, but they both still knew that their boundaries were in place. They might have made an exception and stepped over them once but perhaps the only reason they'd both felt safe to do that was because they both knew they had that safe space to step back into.

Tom would never be ready to abandon that safe space, and Laura? Well, she had Harry to care for and he was the centre of her world. Even if she was prepared to risk her own heart and look for more in her life, Tom was quite sure she would never do anything that might risk Harry's happiness. Especially now, when it seemed that he was going to have a second chance at a real future.

As the days had passed, with Harry coming out of Intensive Care and Laura able to share his room in the paediatric ward, any anxiety that their friendship had been damaged by that one-off night of physical comfort had gradually evaporated completely. And that was making Tom's life exactly how he wanted it to be.

Hey…' Joe looked up as someone called a greeting from where the stairs from ground level led into this staffroom area of the Aratika Rescue Base. 'Maggie… this is a surprise.'

'Oh…' Shirley, the rescue base's volunteer house-keeper, dropped what she was doing at the kitchen bench and rushed towards Maggie, wiping her hands on her apron. 'You've brought darling Bella in to visit.' She held out her arms. 'May I?'

'Of course.' Maggie handed over three-month-old Bella. 'Gotta get a cuddle from Nana Shirley, don't we?' She headed towards the table. 'What have you guys been up to, then?'

'Look at that…' Joe pushed the ECG across the table to his wife. 'From a middle-aged man who had a GCS of less than eight when we arrived on scene.'

'Infarct? No…' Maggie frowned. 'It's too wide-spread. Pericarditis?' She caught Joe's gaze. 'Tell me more. What was he doing before he got sick?'

'Good question,' Tom said. 'He was climbing up a ladder to clean out the gutters on his house.'

'So he fell off the ladder. Traumatic brain injury?'

'Good guess.'

'But why did he fall? A cardiac event?'

'You could think so. But look at this.' Joe pushed the second ECG graph across the table. 'This was a couple of minutes after we did a rapid sequence intubation because he was so agitated.'

Maggie's eyes widened. 'That's normal.'

'Which is why we can be sure that the ECG changes were due to raised intracranial pressure and not a heart attack.'

Maggie sighed. 'I miss being here,' she said. 'As much as I love being home with Bella, I think I'm nearly ready to come back to work.'

'Did you hear that, Bella?' Shirley kissed Bella's curls as she came closer to the table. She grinned at Maggie. 'Maybe we should start a crèche here. I could look after Bella and Harley.'

Bella's squeak might have been agreement but Shirley clicked her tongue. 'Sick of my cuddles already, darling? Here...say hello to your Uncle Tom.'

Tom didn't have time to protest as he had to take the warm bundle of baby being pressed into his arms. He was aware of a surprised glance coming from Joe's direction and his friend moved, as if to rescue him from the situation, but Tom smiled to let him know it was fine.

Which it totally was.

'Hey, there,' he said to Bella. 'Did you come to see Daddy at work, huh?'

Bella's face crinkled into a toothless grin and Tom felt something melt inside. Not in a poignant, even painful way, as it might have done not so long ago. This felt warm and joyful—the way a baby's smile should always make you feel. As if you could believe for at least a few seconds that the world was a place brim full of hope and happiness.

Wow...he'd come quite a long way in the weeks since Bella had arrived in the world, hadn't he?

'We're on the way to see Laura and Harry,' Maggie said. 'Maybe for the last time in the ward. Fizz tells me that he's getting an ultrasound exam today and, depending on the result, they could be letting him go home tomorrow.'

'So I heard.' Tom was still smiling down at the baby. 'I popped up to the ward yesterday. I found a dinosaur

colouring-in book in the gift shop and I knew Harry
would love that.'

'I'll bet he did.'

Tom didn't say anything. He was busy making faces
at Bella in the hope of eliciting another smile. One like
the smile that had been on Harry's face when he'd seen
the book and the big packet of felt tip pens that had
been his gift?

'Did she tell you whether the pathology results from
the surgery had come back yet?' Maggie sounded anxious. 'I didn't like to ask by text.'

'They did. And they couldn't be better.' Tom took
Bella back towards her mother as she squeaked again.
'Totally clear margins and nothing abnormal in the
gallbladder or the lymph nodes. I think he's going to
be one of the lucky ones.'

'I'll bet Laura thinks she's one of the lucky ones,'
Joe said quietly.

That was so true. For a moment, Tom cuddled Bella
a little more tightly before he handed her over. Because
he could remember that glow that Laura had had when
she'd told him the news. He had felt her relief as if it
was his own and he'd caught that flash of a renewed
hope in the future that he could see in her eyes. The
kind of hope you felt in exactly moments like this,
when you were cradling a small baby in your arms.

'That is such good news.' Maggie took Bella from
Tom. 'Okay, Button, come and give Daddy a kiss and
then we'll go visiting. I can't wait to see how happy
Laura must be.'

Joe was still smiling after he'd bestowed kisses on
both Maggie and Bella but Tom could feel a curious
gaze from Joe coming in his direction after their sur-

prise visitors had gone. It happened again a while later, too, after Shirley had gone home, leaving enough fresh muffins for at least twenty-four hours, and it was so quiet that Joe and Tom were sprawled on the sofas, using the time to catch up on articles in emergency medical journals.

'What's so fascinating?' Tom finally had to ask as the intensity of the stare from Joe made him abandon his reading. 'Have I grown an extra ear or something?'

'There's something different about you,' Joe said. 'I'm trying to figure out what it is.'

'Maybe I need a haircut.'

'Nah…it's something bigger than that. It's your body language or something. You're more…relaxed.'

'I'm always relaxed.'

Joe gave a huff of laughter. 'You know, when we first started working together, I thought you were a bit uptight, to be honest.'

'Cheers…'

'You know what I mean. Reserved. Serious. You didn't smile that much and you kind of stood back. Not clinically—you've always been outstanding in the way you work. It was more that you kind of kept your distance, you know? You had that ability to stay calm in any kind of emergency.'

Tom's grunt was agreement. Of course he knew. He still kept his distance when it came to being too emotionally involved with his patients. You had to, in order to do your best job. You had to be able to stand back and see the bigger picture.

'Anyway…' Joe was sitting up now, on the edge of the couch. Leaning forward, as if what he was saying was important. 'You seem different. You smile more and…'

'And…?'

Joe shrugged, as if he was a little embarrassed. 'You remember the day that Bella was born?'

'Of course. It wasn't that long ago.' And it had also been the day that Laura had brought Harry in to the emergency department and her world had begun to fall apart. It was the day when it had been impossible not to feel that connection with a parent who was possibly facing the end of the world as she knew it.

'I felt like I should have said something to Maggie. I hadn't told her about you losing your family because you said it wasn't something you ever talked about so I figured it was private.'

It had been. Very private. The only person Tom had ever talked to it about, apart from Joe, was Laura.

'I was worried that it might have seemed really insensitive when she asked if you wanted to hold Bella.' Joe said. 'I thought that might have been why you rushed off.'

Tom still didn't say anything. Joe wasn't far off the truth, was he? It had been a flashback kind of moment and he had been grappling with some difficult emotions, like grief and the lingering, painful poignancy of enormous loss.

'But today,' Joe continued, 'you actually looked like you didn't mind at all when Shirley shoved Bella into your arms.'

'I didn't mind,' Tom assured him. 'She's got the best smile in the world, your daughter.'

'It's not just that,' Joe added. 'It's the way you've helped Laura so much since Harry got sick. Helping her shift into that new apartment. Making her your neighbour, even... She wouldn't have even known that apartment was available if you hadn't told her.'

'She's a friend,' Tom said. 'It's what friends do.'

They didn't usually start paying a good whack of their rent behind their backs, though, did they? Tom caught the quizzical look Joe was giving him and had the horrible thought that perhaps Joe somehow knew about that secret arrangement. Or worse, did he know about what had happened between himself and Laura that night he'd stayed so that she wasn't alone in her apartment without Harry? That was the sort of thing girlfriends talked about, wasn't it? If Laura had confided in Maggie, it wasn't hard to imagine that Joe might have found out. He swung his legs off the couch and sat up, rubbing the back of his neck.

'You're still staring at me,' he muttered.

Joe grunted his agreement. 'I was just thinking,' he explained. 'Remembering what you told me when I thought that Maggie and I were just friends. That I'd know if I was in love in with her or not. You said I'd know because it would be like the sun had been turned on in my personal universe. But you know what?'

'What?'

'You were wrong. Or kind of wrong. It was the opposite of that that made me realise how I felt about Maggie.'

'Not sure I follow.'

'You remember that accident she had on her motorbike.'

'Of course. When we arrived on scene and you realised who it was who'd had the accident, I think you looked worse than she did for a while.'

'That was because I knew how much I had to lose. The sun had always been there but I suddenly knew how dark my personal universe would be if I didn't have Maggie in my life any more.'

'Yeah…' Tom had to swallow hard. 'It breaks you, that's for sure.'

'Sorry, mate… I didn't mean to remind you of…'

'Her name was Jenny. And my little boy was called Sam. It's okay, Joe. Yes, it broke me at the time but I've put my life back together since then. Having said that, though, I'm not going there again and that's why my friendship with Laura is nothing like your friendship with Maggie. It's only ever going to be a friendship.'

Joe said nothing. He seemed to be carefully avoiding Tom's gaze at the same time and he could understand why his words might lack credibility, given that Joe's relationship with Maggie had grown from what they had both believed was nothing more than a friendship. For everybody's sake, he needed to make sure that Joe understood exactly where he was coming from. What if Joe got the wrong end of the stick and it got back to Laura via Maggie that maybe Tom was ready for something more in his life? That might have to be the end of their friendship and Tom didn't want that. He really didn't want that.

He blew out a long breath. 'Okay…maybe you're right. I am a bit different.' He found a smile to lighten this heavy atmosphere. 'Not so uptight.'

'You're more involved.' Joe nodded. 'Part of the gang now.' Maybe he wanted to finish a conversation that had become unexpectedly intense.

'That's precisely it. I guess I kept myself to myself for a very long time because, initially, I was too broken to cope with anything else and then it just became a way of life and it felt safe. I was in my own little bubble. And then I saw you and Maggie with Bella and Harry got sick and, somehow, that bubble got a bit bigger all by itself. Big enough to let friends in. But that's as far as it goes. And, hey…who wouldn't want to be part of a gang, when there's tacos involved sometimes?'

Joe grinned. 'True. Mmm… Tacos.'

'I'm getting hungry.'

'Me, too. Shall we check out those muffins Shirley made?'

Tom got to his feet. It felt good to move because it made it easier to stop thinking about how much his life might have been changing without him taking that much notice of it. He wanted to focus on making the most of one of his days at the rescue base and revel in whatever new challenges came his way. He wasn't about to enjoy one of Shirley's excellent muffins just yet, however. Right on cue, as the two men were within reach of the basket, their pagers sounded. They exchanged a glance and a resigned grin and then headed for the door.

Normal.

It was a word that could imply something very ordinary and not very interesting.

It was also a word that could be the best news ever when it came from the specialist who was interpreting the ultrasound results on the examination of Harry's liver.

'He said that everything's looking completely normal.'

'Oh, Laura, that's fantastic news.' Maggie had to

swipe at her eyes and then she sniffed loudly. 'Sorry...'
She looked down to where Bella was lying, sucking
her fist, in her car seat. 'Ever since I became a mum,
I seem to get emotional at the drop of a hat about anything to do with kids.'

'I know what you mean. I reckon when you have a
baby, your heart gets instantly bigger. And softer. You
get used to it, but it's never quite the same.'

'Yeah...' Maggie was picking Bella up. 'You're hungry, aren't you? You don't need to eat your hand.' She
adjusted her top and helped Bella latch onto her breast,
softly stroking her baby's cheek as she settled. 'It's like
falling in love, I think. The whole world just looks so
different, especially in those amazing early days when
you feel like you're floating.'

'Mmm...' Laura had to press her lips together.

She wanted so much to tell Maggie that she was
having trouble keeping her feet firmly on the floor
these days. That she could summon that floating sensation as simply as closing her eyes and letting her mind
drift into thinking about Tom Chapman. She could
usually stop that happening easily enough in the daytime but it was a lot harder when she was alone with
her thoughts during the nights. She wanted to admit
that she suspected she might be falling in love.

Worse, she wanted to confess what had happened
that night when she'd been so strongly advised to take
a short break from the tense atmosphere of the PICU.
They were both the sort of things that you had to tell
your best friend but maybe she didn't want to hear her
own doubts out loud.

That Tom was never going to fall in love again because his heart still belonged to the family he'd so

tragically lost so she needed to let go of that faint hope that things could change in the future. Or that she'd made a terrible mistake in practically begging him to make love to her that night because it had been when she'd been drifting off to sleep in his arms that she'd realised that her love for Tom and the power of her desire for him had coalesced into something huge. That this level of love for someone was way beyond any kind of acceptable emotional connection with a friend.

The only real question, here, was whether it was possible to stop that falling process once it had started. Or had it already gone so far she'd hit bottom with such a bump she was still a bit stunned? Maybe she needed a bit more time to think about that herself.

She had to look away before Maggie lifted her gaze from Bella and could instantly spot that Laura was keeping something hidden, but it was easy to make avoiding eye contact seem perfectly innocent. They were on a couch in the corner of the playroom and she needed to keep an eye on Harry and make sure he wasn't overdoing things, having been out of bed for most of today already. He and his friend Aroha were sitting at a low table on brightly coloured chairs. Aroha had big crayons and was drawing on a large piece of paper. Harry had the colouring-in book Tom had given him yesterday and he was carefully filling in the outline of a Triceratops. Because that had been the dinosaur that he and Tom had had a conversation about?

'Why has he got horns? So he could kill animals and eat them?'

'No...he was a vegetarian. I think he used his horns to protect himself, like when he got into an argument with a T Rex.'

Ooh…there it was again. That floaty sensation, sneaking back during daytime—just because she could actually hear Tom's voice in her head. Not only his words to Harry but the way he'd sounded when she'd shown him the pathology report she had been given.

'Intact liver capsule. Absence of vascular invasion. Negative resection margins... This is the best news ever...'

'I know, right? I don't think I've ever felt this happy.'

She'd come close, though, hadn't she? That night, when she'd taken that break from Harry's bedside, knowing that he was in safe hands and she would be back before he woke up. When she'd been falling into that desperately needed sleep, in the wake of a physical release she hadn't known she'd needed so much. When she'd felt Tom's arms around her and the steady beat of his heart and the way it felt as if her own heart could explode with the amount of love that was filling it. When, for a blissful, albeit short period of time, there had been nothing more that she could possibly need.

Except for those results that had come yesterday, of course. Knowing that Harry's surgery had been so successful. That life could very likely get completely back to normal in the foreseeable future. Or maybe not completely…

Falling in love—if the process couldn't be interrupted—presented a bit of a problem. Laura needed Tom in her life for Harry's sake as well as her own because every fatherless child needed a role model and she couldn't imagine anyone better than Tom, but there was only one way that was going to happen, which was to keep things the way they had been. A friendship and nothing more. She'd known that from the moment she'd woken up to find that Tom had slipped out of her bed while she had been so deeply asleep and he'd gone to sleep on the couch.

It hadn't been hard to pick up on how uncomfortable he was feeling as they sped through what needed to be done before heading back to the hospital. It was obvious that Tom thought he was going to have to spell out why they could never be anything more than friends and that perhaps they had made a bit of mess of things last night but he couldn't find a way to broach the subject. The tension had quietly notched up as they failed to find a way into the conversation that had to happen.

Laura had rescued him as they'd walked back to the Royal. She'd taken a deep breath and told him how it had been exactly what she'd needed but that she never expected it to happen again. That it was pretty much out of bounds for a normal friendship.

There it was again. That word.

Anyway, she'd also told him that nobody else needed to know so that meant she really couldn't tell Maggie because it would feel as if she was breaking a promise. If it got to the point where she couldn't cope with her secret, at least she knew she had friends she could turn to but it felt fine for now. She could do this.

She needed to focus on her son and make sure that his recovery and the final chemotherapy he was going to need went as well as it possibly could. She could be friends with Tom and keep the knowledge of what it was like to be that much closer to him a memory that she could revisit when she needed an escape, perhaps. A bit of a fantasy about what life could have been like if things were different. When she wanted to feel special. Gorgeous, even…

'What is it?'

Laura hadn't felt her friend's gaze on her. She hadn't realised she was smiling.

'Oh, I'm just happy. Seeing Harry like this. Knowing that we're going to go home tomorrow.'

'Is there anything you need? I could do a grocery run or something for you.' Maggie eased a now drowsy Bella into an upright position on her shoulder and began rubbing her back. 'Or I could come and stay with Harry soon and give you a bit of a break.'

'Come and visit anytime,' Laura said, 'but I don't think I'll be needing a break. I'm going to enjoy every minute with Harry at home.'

Again, it was almost on the tip of her tongue to tell Maggie what had happened the last time she'd taken a break from watching her son. At least that couldn't happen with him at home again so maybe the memory would begin to fade soon. She could stamp on those errant thoughts that she might be wrong. That maybe Tom wanted it to happen again as much as she did. She wanted so badly to feel like it was safe to love this man, but it wasn't, was it? She could end up getting badly hurt.

She had to at least try to protect herself by keeping things real. Nothing was going to change in the future because Tom would never want that. If she started to think otherwise, she just needed to remind herself of that night when they'd almost, accidentally kissed and he couldn't get away fast enough afterwards. Or she could tap into that tension the morning after they'd made love. Yep…that was extremely effective. Laura could feel herself frowning now as she pushed away her own uncomfortable feelings.

'There's online shopping.' Maybe Maggie thought she was worrying about getting groceries. 'I've been using that since Bella arrived and it's great. You just order everything and it gets delivered to your doorstep. I'm sure Tom would help carry it all inside.'

'Mmm...' No. Laura didn't want to think about Tom coming into her apartment with grocery bags in his hands—as if he was a part of her everyday life. So she said the first thing that came into her head to try and change the subject. 'Did you know that he eats micro-wave meals? How sad is that? I've told him I'm going to teach him how to cook a spaghetti bolognaise.'

Uh-oh... The way Maggie was looking at her sug-gested that there were cogs whirring in her friend's brain. That she was adding two and two together and coming up with a sum a lot greater than four.

Laura shook her head firmly. 'We're just friends.'

'Right...' Maggie's grin widened as Bella burped loudly. 'Now, where have I heard that before? Oh, yeah... That's exactly what Joe and I tried to con-vince ourselves we were. Before we realised that we'd already fallen in love.' She shifted her gaze to where Harry was still sitting, colouring in his picture. 'I guess the timing isn't right, though, is it? You're not going to go off and start dating anyone while Harry needs your undivided attention.'

She tucked her sleeping baby back into the car seat. 'I'd better get going. Joe texted to ask if Tom could come around for dinner tonight. For some reason, they've both got a hankering for tacos so I'll have to drop in to the supermarket. Didn't think to order taco shells online this week, that's for sure. I don't think we've had tacos since the day you moved apartments.

Hey…maybe you could teach Tom how to make them, too. I'm sure he's going to love having a private cooking tutor.'

Laura was smiling now. 'Stop trying to start rumours. And don't you dare say anything to Tom or he'll regret ever suggesting that I become his neighbour.'

'My lips are sealed.' There was something rather serious in Maggie's gaze as she leaned in to give Laura a hug. 'You can tell me anything, you know. They'd still be sealed.'

Laura opened her mouth to tell her that there was nothing to tell but the words refused to come out. So she just hugged her friend instead.

CHAPTER NINE

THIS WAS GREAT.

A new normal.

It had taken a few weeks but Laura and Tom had found the space they could both be happy sharing. A solid friendship that meant they could stop and chat for a few minutes if they happened to be heading out or arriving home at the same time. They could work together, having lost none of their ability to communicate with each other so easily. Laura knew this because she'd had her first shift back in the emergency department since Harry had started back at school after his surgery and it had been a real joy. A sure sign that life was getting back to normal.

But maybe even better than the old normal because she still had Tom in her life and they had shored up the boundaries that meant that night together had been forgotten. Well, not forgotten as far as Laura was concerned, of course, but it was in a manageable place. She was coping so well, in fact, that she'd been totally relaxed in finally following up on that invitation to give Tom a cooking lesson.

So, here they were in her kitchen and the tempt-

ing aroma of frying onions and garlic was filling her
kitchen.

'You can add the minced meat soon.'

'Okay.' Tom had the sleeves of his sweatshirt pushed
up. 'It's beef, yeah?'

His hands brushed Laura's as he took the package
of meat but she barely registered the tingle. Maybe because it was so much easier to control something like
that when Harry was nearby. He was currently crawl-
ing around the floor of the living area, setting up the
tracks for his model train set. Laura went back to the
celery and carrots she was dicing.

'Beef and pork,' she told Tom. 'It's a lot better than
beef on its own. I have a secret ingredient too that you
won't find in most recipes and you certainly won't find
it in a microwaveable version.'

'Oh?' Tom raised an eyebrow as he looked over his
shoulder. 'I assume you're going to tell me what it is?
Friends get to share secrets, don't they?'

'Sure…' But Laura had to drag her gaze away from
Tom's. Oh, man… Did he not realise exactly what secret they shared that was going to pop instantly into her
head? Maybe this wasn't quite as easy as she'd hoped
it would be. She covered up her avoidance of his gaze
by reaching for another package.

'It's bacon,' she said. 'Chop a couple of rashers up
finely and put it in with the onion and garlic. Better if
it goes in before the mince, actually.'

'No worries.' Tom still sounded completely relaxed
so he clearly hadn't been reminded of anything that
could become awkward. 'And then we put the veg-
gies in?'

'Yes. And the tomatoes and stock and a bit of red

wine. I'm not sure if we should use the bottle you brought, though. It looks like a very good wine.'

'I watched a cooking show once,' Tom said. 'And the chef said, if you wouldn't want to drink it, don't cook with it.'

'I don't usually put any in when it's just me and Harry.'

'Maybe we should just drink it, then?'

Tom's smile had a mischievous edge now and it made something melt deep inside Laura. Something very warm and...and safe, she realised. She could stop worrying about feeling things that might not be appropriate because surely they would fade eventually. They had to, because this friendship—and this feeling of safety—was too precious to lose.

She smiled back. 'I'll find the glasses. You keep cooking.'

By the time she had uncorked the bottle and poured them both a glass, Tom had added everything to the saucepan.

'It just needs to simmer for a while now. Sit down and enjoy your wine. I'll tidy up in here so that we'll be able to eat at the table. Or, if you've got anything you need to do at home, I can give you a yell when it's ready to eat?'

'Noo... I want Tom to come and play trains with me. He promised...'

Laura blinked. She'd had no idea that Harry had been listening in to their conversation. 'Did he?'

Tom took a sip from his glass. 'Well, I did say it looked like fun when I saw him emptying that box. But it is a long time since I played trains. I might have forgotten how.'

'It's all right,' Harry's tone was reassuring. 'I'll show you. It's not very hard. But we have to build a bridge first, okay?'

Tom looked at the fistful of train tracks Harry was holding up to show him. He looked at the wine glass in his hand and then he looked at Laura.

Her smile widened. 'Take it with you,' she advised. 'You might need it.'

Harry had been right. It wasn't hard to play trains at all. It was actually surprisingly enjoyable.

Maybe that was because it felt good to be here, instead of being alone in his own apartment, waiting for a frozen dinner to warm up. Not that he minded his own company, Tom reminded himself. Far from it—he'd learned to appreciate it over the last few years but it was nice to have a change sometimes and being with friends was something special. Like that taco dinner he'd had with Maggie and Joe just before Harry had been discharged from hospital. This evening, it was great to see Harry looking so much better and, he had to admit, the smell coming from Laura's kitchen was so much better than any boxed version of spaghetti bolognaise.

The wine he was able to snatch an occasional sip from as he built a bridge, put curves into a straight line that was about to take the track into the kitchen where Laura was busy cleaning up the mess he'd made cooking, positioned a station and then started pushing engines and carriages around, was making the whole experience even more enjoyable. Tom was feeling a lot more relaxed than he had since...well, since the last time he'd been in this apartment with Laura, that was for sure. Even thinking about that awkward 'morning after' was enough to provoke a beat of…what was it, exactly? Wariness?

It was another good thing about this evening. To have the confirmation that Laura had been being completely honest when she'd said that night was just a one-off and that she'd never expect it to happen again. Ever since then, she hadn't given the slightest hint that she wanted more than a normal kind of friendship from him. Which was excellent, because it made a neighbourly evening like this possible.

'What's that, Harry?' Tom peered at the small black object Harry was slotting into an open train carriage.

'It's a seal.'

'What, a seal that goes in the sea and makes a noise like this?'

Tom flapped his bent arms like flippers and did his best to mimic the barking sound that seals make. Harry laughed out loud and copied Tom and from the corner of his eye Tom could see that the sound had brought Laura into the archway between the kitchen and living area. She was already smiling but clearly wanted to see what was causing so much amusement. The light behind her was stronger than in this room and it lit up that gorgeous auburn hair of hers in a glow that was an almost perfect match to that rust-coloured sweatshirt she was wearing again.

Which took him straight back to that evening when she'd come out of the shower and worse than that∴ much worse than that…it took him straight back to what had happened not long after that. He could remember so clearly the softness and taste of Laura's lips and the perfect curves of her body. He could actually feel the echoes of the touch of her hands on his skin that was so delicate, it was hard to believe they could ignite that kind of fire in their wake…

Oh, man… Tom was grateful for the noise of small plastic bricks cascading from the large box as Harry emptied his supplies onto the floor because the sound drowned thoughts that were escalating rapidly out of control.

'I've got a whole zoo,' he told Tom. 'Look, here's a lion…and a giraffe. What sort of noise does a giraffe make?'

'I'm not sure,' Tom admitted. 'But why don't you put them under the bridge? That way, the people in the train can see them as they go on their trip.'

'You'll have to be quick,' Laura said. 'Dinner's going to be ready soon.'

By the time dinner was ready, Tom was confident he had those disturbing reminders of that night with Laura under control. It was hardly likely that his body was going to let him forget that it had experienced the extraordinary release of sex for the first time in so long. After all, it had been a wake-up call to be as affected as he had been by that "almost kiss". Perhaps he'd been right in thinking that he needed to find someone to share a relationship like a "friends with benefits" kind of thing.

For one, crazy moment, Tom found himself wondering if Laura might be interested in a relationship like that and he must have had a strange expression on his face because her eyebrows shot up when she caught his glance.

'What's up?'

'That's not spaghetti.' He focused on the large bowl

on the table. The pasta that had been mixed in with the sauce he'd made earlier was a lot flatter and thicker than spaghetti. 'I thought that's what bolognaise was all about.'

'It's tagliatelle. It's better than spaghetti because more of the sauce can stick to it. Plus, it's easier for small people to eat.' Laura was serving some into a bowl for Harry. 'Is that enough, sweetheart?' she asked. 'And do you want cheese on top?'

Tom watched her making sure that Harry had everything he needed before she served herself and the way she kept an eye on him throughout the meal. No...he'd known all along that Laura wasn't the type of woman that would be happy with casual sex as part of a friendship. She was such a loving person and such a wonderful mother. Someone to whom family was everything and that family was her precious son.

Her smile was amused but with a twist of resignation at the moment because Harry was using his fingers to try and wrap the pasta around his fork and he had such a fierce expression of concentration with his brow furrowed like that. When his fork was overfull, trying to eat it left sauce all over his face and hands. Now he looked worried because he knew he'd made a mess, but when he looked up at his mother he clearly knew he wasn't in trouble and his face lit up with a grin.

'I'll get a cloth,' Laura said. 'Don't move, monkey.'

It was Harry's grin that did it. The happiness of someone who knew they were loved unconditionally. Or maybe it was because he'd been thinking about the bond of family, and memories were never that far away if his guard was down. Faded memories that were almost dreamlike now and the emotions they stirred were more like longing than sadness. Whatever. It was Laura that had that bond, not him. And it was not something he ever wanted to have again himself. It was just as well that this meal was nearly finished. He could excuse himself and go home very soon. Tom used a piece of crusty bread to mop up the last of the sauce on his plate.

'That was absolutely delicious,' he told Laura. 'I can't believe I cooked most of it myself.'

She threw him a sideways glance as she went towards Harry with a damp cloth. 'Maggie reckons I should teach you to make tacos next time.'

Harry ducked his head to try and avoid having the sauce wiped off his face. 'I want tacos for my party,' he said. He peered under his mother's arm. 'Are you coming to my party, Tom?'

'Um… You're having a party? Is it your birthday?'

'Not yet,' Laura said. 'And the party's a wee way off, as well, but we're planning to celebrate the end of chemo. It's going to be in one of the cafés in the Royal so it might be just cake and not tacos but that makes it easy for Harry's friends from the ward to come, like Aroha. And Fizz—and maybe you—will be able to come for a while even if you're both working.'

'That's certainly something worth celebrating…' Although Tom wasn't sure it would be a good idea to attend the party, as if his inclusion in his neighbour's special occasions was automatic.

'Mummy says I can have a special present because I've been very, very brave.'

'That's true,' Tom agreed.

'He hasn't decided what he wants yet,' Laura put in.

'I think it's a toss-up between a bike and a new tablet to play computer games on.'

'No.' Harry's headshake was firm. 'I've decided now.'

'Oh?' Laura was still smiling as she began collecting empty plates. 'What's it going to be, then, this special present?'

'Tom.'

It felt like time stopped for an instant of confusion. Tom was halfway up from his chair. Laura froze with a stack of plates in mid-air. They were both staring at Harry.

'I want Tom,' he said. 'I want him to be my daddy.'

Oh...no... No, no, no...

The new normal had just been destroyed by a few innocent words from a six-year-old boy.

Laura had to fix this. And fast. If that was even possible. The look on Tom's face was...

Heartbreaking, that's what it was.

He'd been a daddy once. To a little boy who would be about the same age as Harry if he was still alive. Her son's words must have felt like he was having his heart ripped out and someone was stomping on it.

'Harry...' She tried to make it sound like this was all a joke. 'That's a funny thing to say.'

'Why?'

'Because...because you can't give someone a person for a present, can you?' Laura knew her laughter sounded forced. 'How would you wrap them up?'

'But...' Harry's lower lip was protruding—a sure sign that he was prepared to go into battle for what he wanted.

'Tom's our friend,' Laura added firmly. 'And that's special enough, isn't it?'

Harry was still scowling.

'How 'bout you go and tidy up those building bricks?' Laura said a little desperately. 'When you've done that, you can have some ice cream for dessert.'

Harry slid down from his chair and reluctantly took a couple of steps before looking back at Tom. 'Please will you help me?'

'Sorry, buddy.' Tom was out of his chair, as well. 'I need to help your mum with the dishes and then... ah...it's time for me to go home.'

He caught Laura's glance for no more than a split second. Just long enough for her to know that he was finding this as excruciatingly embarrassing as she was. This was far worse than the awkwardness of that morning after they'd slept together. Tom picked up the serving bowls from the table and turned towards the bench.

Harry wasn't giving up. 'Why?'

'Because I have lots of homework to do.' Tom put the leftovers down beside where Laura had deposited the plates.

'And because it's going to be your bedtime very soon.' Laura hoped her over-the-shoulder smile at Tom was both an apology and reassurance as she turned on the hot tap over the sink. 'I don't need any help with the dishes,' she told him. 'You did most of the cooking so you're excused.'

'You sure?'

'Absolutely...' She took a deep breath and lowered her voice. 'And... I'm sorry for that. He had fun playing with you, that's all. And he doesn't understand. He's just...'

'A kid. I know...' Tom was smiling back at her. 'It's okay, Laura. Forget it. But I do have quite a lot of work to be getting on with, if you're sure about the dishes. I've been meaning to write up a case report on some interesting ECG changes from raised intracranial pressure we captured a while back.'

'Go...' Laura's smile widened in relief at the normal tone of Tom's voice. 'And don't let Harry talk you into helping on your way past.'

She kept an eye on her son as Tom negotiated a path through the scattered bricks. She saw the way he leaned down to touch Harry's head in farewell. It would have been a hair ruffle but it would be quite a while before her boy's hair grew back enough to be ruffled.

The lump in her throat as she turned back to rinsing the plates was big enough to be painful. Hearing the sound of her front door closing behind Tom only seemed to make it worse. It wasn't the embarrassment of Harry having said something that unintentionally could have upset Tom that was the worst thing about how this cooking lesson and dinner had ended.

No. It was something far worse.

It was how Laura had felt when she'd heard Harry utter those words. The knowledge that it was what *she* wanted—probably a whole lot more than Harry did. There was no getting around the fact that she was completely in love with Tom but she'd known all along that the only way to keep him in her life was as a friend and she'd believed that could be enough. Now she knew that it wasn't enough. She would always long to have Tom in her life in the closest possible way. Not simply as a daddy for her son. She wanted him as her life partner. Someone she could love with her whole heart and soul for the rest of her life.

No…make that *would* love. Laura had another attempt to swallow that lump that was making it hard to breathe.

How she felt about Tom Chapman wasn't about to change.

Ever.

Writing up a case report hadn't actually been on Tom's agenda that evening but it had been a brainwave. A sure-fire way of clearing his head from what felt like a minor storm of unwelcome emotions that were still spinning around inside his skull even after he was safely alone in his own apartment.

Shock waves, that's what they were.

Partly because Harry's words had tapped into memories that he'd almost forgotten he had. Sam, as a toddler, saying 'Daddy' for the first time and the tears of joy in both his and Jenny's eyes as they'd heard him. That family hug…

That longing that he'd already been observing during that dinner had suddenly grown the sharp edges of reality because his memories of the family he'd once had were simply that. Memories that, more and more these days, had a dreamlike quality. Being with Laura and Harry was different. It was very, very real and there he'd been sitting at the table with them as he'd become so aware of that reality. He'd been playing with Harry and that train set only a short time ago.

Just like a father would.

He'd become far closer to both of them than he'd ever intended when he'd been drawn into helping with the crisis in their lives. When he'd had that apparently random thought of Laura being a "friend with benefits" this evening, it hadn't just been the idea of casual sex that had been appealing, had it?

Subconsciously, at least, it had been that whole concept of family. Of belonging. Of loving and being loved by others…? Certainly, if he let this go any further, Tom would be in danger of falling in love with both Laura and Harry and reaching to have that joy of family in his life again, and he knew what that meant. It meant having the other side of that coin. The risk of losing everything again. Of having your entire world destroyed.

Nobody thought it was going to happen to them but Tom knew that it *could* happen. He knew that it felt unsurvivable when it did. That putting the pieces of a life back together again to that extent was not something you could do more than once. The very thought of facing something like that again gave him a prickle down his spine that could only be caused by fear.

He'd learned how to protect himself so how the hell had his defences crumbled to such an extent?

More importantly, what was he going to do about strengthening them again?

CHAPTER TEN

IT WAS BECOMING a habit.

Sometimes with grocery bags at her feet, or Harry's schoolbag or just the two of them because they'd gone for a walk, there was always that moment when Laura was fishing for her keys in her handbag or her pocket and she'd know that Harry had turned around.

That he was staring at the front door of Tom's apartment. That the usual questions were about to be asked.

'Is Tom home, Mummy? Can I knock on the door?'

'I don't think so, hon.' Laura hated the pang it always gave her, trying to shelter Harry. It didn't matter if she was hurt by Tom's stepping back after that cooking lesson that had ended so disastrously but it was one thing for her to feel hurt and quite another that Harry was affected by it. 'It was really busy at work today and he has lots of sick people to look after.'

'He looked after me when I was sick.'

'Mmm…' Laura smiled as she fitted the key in the lock. 'He sure did.'

'I think I might be feeling sick again today.'

That beat of alarm was always going to be there. 'What kind of sick?'

'I think my tummy hurts.'

'You *think* it hurts?' Laura lifted Harry's cap off his head so that she could see his face clearly. He wasn't pale and he avoided her gaze by looking over his shoulder at Tom's door again, which was a good clue that he wasn't actually feeling sick—he just wanted an excuse to see Tom. Laura's suspicion was confirmed when he reached up and took his dinosaur cap out of her hands. 'Tom gave me my hat.'

'Mmm...' The sound was a little strangled.

That cap. No, all those caps. That had been the moment that falling in love process had started, even if she hadn't recognised it at the time—when she'd seen all those children coming out of school wearing the red dinosaur caps. Being part of "Harry's club".

Those feelings were never going to change but she couldn't blame Tom for having put his barriers up again. Not that he wasn't perfectly friendly still, but it reminded her of what he'd been like in the past. Before Harry had got sick. When he had kept his distance from people.

Becoming close enough to be considered a friend had been a privilege but, without realising it, Laura had let it go too far. She'd read too much into the connection she thought they had between them. He'd made it feel as if it was safe to love someone like this and what made it so much worse was that she hadn't protected Harry enough. He loved Tom, too.

Now she was following his lead and keeping things light and friendly because that had worked once before, hadn't it? After the awkwardness of having slept together, they'd managed to rescue their friendship and it had seemed even stronger than before but it appeared that it was going to take longer this time. Harry's notion that Tom could be his daddy had opened old wounds and it was no wonder that he needed to protect himself and that he needed some space. Maybe, one day, they could relax in each other's company again. If not, they could get used to that loss gradually, at least.

Harry was following her inside. 'I still like wearing it but I don't need it any more, do I, Mummy?'

'Not really. Your hair is growing back fast. It's great, isn't it?' Just a few weeks after his last chemotherapy session, Harry's scalp was covered with a fine, dark fuzz—so soft that it brought a lump to Laura's throat every time she stroked it.

She was the luckiest person on earth, she thought in those moments. All test results were coming back indicating that Harry had won this battle and, apart from regular check-ups, he was unlikely to need any further treatment. He was still a little underweight and got tired more easily than he used to but he was happy to be back at school and happy when he was at home—apart from those hopeful gazes at Tom's front door, as if he was going to see his hero appear while he watched.

Had he forgotten to shut the front door on purpose, perhaps, so that he would notice when Tom came home today? Having dropped his schoolbag in the middle of the living room floor, Harry had vanished into his bedroom so Laura went to shut the door but just before she closed it, she could hear two people coming in through the apartment building's main entrance. A woman was speaking clearly.

'...so it's only one-bedroom, but it does have a sun-room that opens into the garden and can be used as a second bedroom. I believe that's what the current tenant is using it for.'

Laura held the door just before pushing it shut. Were they talking about her apartment?

'And when are you planning to put it on the market?'

'Not immediately. We've only lost Mum recently and there's a bit to be decided in her estate but I knew you were looking for an investment. If you come up-stairs, you can get a good view of the whole complex. I don't want to disturb my tenant yet and I would prefer to be able to tell her that it might only be the landlord that's going to change.'

They were going past Laura's door now, heading for the stairs.

'What's the rental return like, Carla?'

'Not bad at all. But that's another reason I don't want to approach my tenant yet. She's got a friend who's secretly paying half her rent.' The woman's voice was fading. 'Her little boy's got cancer...how sad is that?'

Very softly, Laura let the door click shut.

Her first thought was that her landlord was wrong. Harry didn't have cancer any more.

Her second thought, as she kicked off her shoes and sank down onto the edge of the couch, felt like a body blow. She had a friend who was paying half her rent? There was only one person who could possibly be doing that and it wasn't hard to summon a memory that should have made her suspicious all along.

*'You're in a pretty exclusive part of town, Tom. I'd
never be able to afford to live there.'*

*'You might be surprised. I think the rent is quite
reasonable, actually.'*

But why would he have done that?

Because he'd felt sorry for her?

Of course he had. That had been where their connection had come from in the first place. He had been
through the agony of losing his own child and, at that
time, he'd known that Laura could be facing the same,
dreadful loss. And what else had he said? Oh, yeah...
He'd offered to be a living donor for Harry because he
hadn't been able to do something like that for his own
son. Had he gone too far in helping them find a new
place to live because of that same need to help another
little boy who was facing a crisis?

Support was acceptable from friends. Welcome. But
charity? It made Laura feel as if she had failed in some
way. That someone thought that she wasn't capable of
protecting her own child well enough.

And she felt...deceived. She had believed Tom when
he'd told her what the rent was. She'd trusted him so
why would the idea that he might be lying by omission have occurred to her?'

What else had he told her that she shouldn't have
believed?

That she was super-smart? Gorgeous? They were
just words. He didn't want to be anything more than
her friend. He'd only made love to her because she'd
begged him to...and because he'd felt so sorry for her?

How stupid had it been to think that a perfect apartment like this, in this part of town, would have been

so affordable? About as stupid as moving in next door to Tom Chapman.

Oh…those echoes from the past were never that far away, were they?

You're so stupid…

Just get out of my way…

Laura pushed herself to her feet. She needed to get out of her own way right now and think of what needed to be done. Like a visit to the bank first thing tomorrow morning to organise a loan that would not only enable her to pay Tom back every cent he'd spent on her rent but give her enough time to find a more affordable place for her and Harry to live.

He'd probably be delighted to know that she would be living further away. It would make it a lot easier to avoid any awkward moments with either her or Harry. Oh, man…had she really believed that it was safe to open her heart to loving someone again? Tears weren't far away as Laura began to wonder if a fresh start might be the best plan despite how hard it would be to leave her friends behind. A new life in another city, perhaps?

It was partly that tears were blurring her vision that made it difficult to see the small, plastic bricks scattered over the living room carpet, but it was because she had kicked off her shoes that Laura suffered the pain of standing on one of the bricks that was out of all proportion to its size.

'*Ow…*' It was the last straw of too many upsetting thoughts and feelings. '*Harry*?' She hadn't sounded this cross with him in a very, very long time. 'Come out here right now, please, and tidy up these bricks.' Her voice was still rising as she marched towards the bathroom. 'Get them *all* in their box by the time I've had my shower and put the box in the hall cupboard. If I see a single one of those bricks again today, they're all going in the rubbish.'

As part of the Helicopter Emergency Medical Service, Tom was well used to the kind of drama that involved a lot of emergency vehicles, flashing lights and people in uniforms. Quite often, when they were arriving at an accident scene on the motorway, for example, it looked like they were landing in the middle of an action movie with numerous people and vehicles from the police, fire and ambulance service.

It was not something he was used to seeing, however, when he was arriving home in the evening after a hectic day in the emergency department of the Royal. Not that there were any ambulances or fire engines but there was a police car and a van with flashing lights looking even more dramatic due to the fading daylight, and there were people in uniforms, one of whom was blocking the gateway, which forced Tom to stop. Behind this officer he could see a handler with a police dog that seemed to be being used to search the grounds of his apartment building.

'What's going on?' Tom asked. 'Someone been burgled? Or attacked?'

'Do you live here, sir?'

'Yes, I do.'

'We've got a child missing.'

'Oh, my God...' Tom felt his heart miss a beat. '*Harry*?'

'You know him?'

'Yes. His mother's my neighbour. A good friend...'

Not that he'd been a very good friend recently, had he? He hadn't even seen Harry in days. A week or more probably and that had only been a quick hi as they'd passed in the hallway. It had been so much easier to step back into safe territory and the longer they'd left it, the more uncomfortable it had seemed to become to address what was causing the growing distance between them.

'Where *is* Laura?'

'She's inside. She wants to be out searching but it's best if we do that. Especially as it doesn't look like he's on the grounds anymore.'

But Tom wasn't listening. He had pushed past the officer and was heading inside at a run. The front door of the building was open. So was Laura's door. Tom walked in without knocking. He walked past two police officers who were in the living area of Laura's apartment and straight into the kitchen where he could see Laura sitting at the table, with photographs spread out in front of her. She looked up as he reached the archway separating the kitchen and living area and by the time Tom had taken two more steps, she was on her feet.

And in his arms. They both spoke at the same time.

'I'm so sorry...' What for, Tom wasn't quite sure. For not being home earlier today so that he could have somehow prevented whatever had happened?

That Laura was facing yet another crisis in her life?

For the way he'd been keeping his distance from her? And from Harry?

'It's all my fault...' Laura was sobbing. 'I shouted at Harry for leaving his bricks on the floor. I was only in the shower for a few minutes but when I came out, he was gone…'

'He can't have gone far.' Tom tightened his hold on Laura. 'We'll find him.'

'I thought he'd just be hiding because I'd told him off. I was sure he'd be inside those bushes near the gate waiting for…waiting for you to get home. He wanted to knock on your door when we got home but I said he couldn't because you'd still be at work and…and…'

Something squeezed painfully in Tom's chest. He knew that there was a bigger reason that Laura wouldn't let Harry knock on his door. She didn't want him being a nuisance. Or upsetting him by saying something that might remind him that he'd lost his own son.

'And he said he felt sick.' Laura was still speaking quickly, as if she needed to tell Tom everything as quickly as possible. 'That his tummy was hurting and he remembered that you'd looked after him that first day when I brought him into ED…'

Tom could remember that, too. So clearly. That had been when he'd felt the first connection with Laura. When the urge to protect her had come from nowhere and had only grown stronger over the last few months. Right now, it was the strongest it had ever been and it wasn't only for Laura. He needed to be able to protect Harry, as well.

Somehow…

'What if he *is* sick?' Laura's voice was muffled, probably by a combination of tears and her face being pressed against his chest. 'And *where* is he? I looked everywhere I could think of and asked everyone I could find but nobody had seen him. Someone said

I needed to call the police and that was when I got really scared and that's...' Laura gulped in a breath. '...hours ago now.'

'Just over an hour.' One of the police officers came into the kitchen. 'I know it feels like a lot longer.' She gestured towards the table. 'Have you found the most recent photograph of Harry?'

It felt like Laura was reluctant to move out of Tom's arms. He felt the same way. He didn't want to let her go. Ever. Could she see that when she looked up and held his gaze for a long moment? It felt like she could. For just a heartbeat, it felt as if any barriers between them had simply evaporated. But then Tom could see a flicker of something else. Wariness? Mistrust, even? He could feel the way she was gathering her strength from some inner resources as she pulled out of his arms and moved towards the table.

'This one's older.' Laura picked up a photograph. 'But this is his school uniform and that's what he's still wearing as far as I know.'

Tom was very familiar with that uniform of dark shorts and long socks and the blue polo shirt. He'd seen Harry wearing it dozens of times. He'd seen a whole school wearing it that day he'd taken the box of dinosaur caps there.

'And this one is the most recent, taken when he was in the oncology day unit having his last chemo session. But he's got more hair now. It's like a very short buzz cut.'

Really? It was great news that Harry's hair was already growing back but why hadn't he noticed that? Because he hadn't been looking, Tom reminded himself. He'd been avoiding a six-year-old boy who'd wanted to knock at his door. That squeeze in his chest ramped up a notch.

'He might be wearing a cap, though,' Laura told the police officer. 'I'll have a look to see if it's in his room.'

'What sort of cap is it?'

'A red one.' Tom answered for Laura. 'A red base-ball cap and it's got a green dinosaur on the front. A T Rex.' He was following Laura into Harry's bedroom. It wasn't that he thought he could be helpful in search-ing for the cap, he just needed to stay close to her. Be-cause the way she had just pulled away from him was so disturbing?

Harry's bedroom was untidy. The contents of his schoolbag were scattered over the floor amongst toys and books. The doors of a cupboard were open and the shelves full of clothes. Laura glanced over her shoulder as she completed a first, quick glance around the room.

'You don't need to stay. I can manage.'

'I know you can.' Laura's courage and ability to manage the worst of situations had been one of the first things he'd admired so much about her.

'Really?' There was a catch in Laura's voice as she dropped to her knees to peer under Harry's bed. 'Is that why you decided it would be a good idea to pay half my rent behind my back?'

Tom froze. How on earth had Laura found out about that? And why had it had to happen at the worst pos-sible time?

'You lied to me, Tom.' Laura's voice was muffled but he could hear how much it had hurt her. She had trusted him and he'd let her down.

'I didn't *lie*, exactly…'

'You didn't tell me the whole truth and that's pretty

much the same as lying.' Laura scrambled to her feet again. 'How can I trust anything you've ever said to me?'

'Because...because I'd never do anything to hurt you, Laura. You *or* Harry. Because... I love you.'

Laura gave her head a sharp shake, reaching into the shelves of the cupboard to pull at clothing in case the cap had been shoved between things.

'As a friend, sure. At a hint of anything more, you can't run away fast enough. I can't walk that kind of tightrope—especially right now.' She turned towards Tom and the pain in her eyes was shocking. 'I don't know where my son is, Tom. I'm *so* scared. And when you're this scared, you don't want to be with a friend you can't trust. Who can just push you out of their lives the way you can.'

Her words hit Tom like a physical blow. Hurting her had been the last thing he'd wanted to happen but it had. He *had* been trying to love her simply as a friend but he'd been lying about that, too, hadn't he? To himself as much as Laura.

They both seemed to be caught in one of those moments when time slowed and everything else became part of the background—even the terrible anxiety of not knowing where Harry was. Somehow, Tom had to let Laura know that she could trust him.

'I wanted to protect you,' he said quietly. 'I just didn't want to fall in love with you because I never wanted to risk loving and losing people I love that much again. But it happened when I wasn't watching... when I wasn't being careful enough...'

He couldn't tell if Laura was even absorbing what he was telling her. The words, even though they were coming straight from his heart, were astonishing to him and he was the one uttering them. Laura shook her head again, as if dismissing anything that wasn't relevant to what was happening right now, and after another rapid scan she left the room. 'It's not there,' she told the police officer.

Another officer came into the apartment. 'We haven't managed to pick up a useful trail with the dog yet. Have you thought any more about where he might think to go? Has he got any friends who live nearby?'

'The only person we really know around here is Tom,' Laura said. 'All his friends live up in the valley near his school.'

Tom swallowed hard. He'd been the one to persuade Laura to move into this apartment block. He'd made it easy for her by making sure she could afford it. He'd been so impressed with her attitude to life's difficulties—that you had to take the cards you were dealt and play the best possible game—but he'd been the one to put that card in her hand. He'd thought he was protecting her. Helping them both, but had he actually made life more difficult?

And Laura had been right—he had lied to her by omission. It was something else to add to the emotional storm he was currently experiencing.

'There's Aroha,' Laura added then, as if inspiration had struck. 'She's his friend from hospital and they just adore each other.'

'Could he have tried to go there? Does he know the way?' The police officer was reaching for the radio clipped to his shoulder. 'I'll get someone onto it.'

'We have walked there a few times but he's only six…he's scared to cross huge roads by himself. And besides, he knows that Aroha went home about the same time he did after his surgery. Ages ago… Oh, I've just thought of somewhere else his cap might be— in the hall cupboard.' Laura walked towards the front door of her apartment, opened the cupboard and bent down to search at floor level.

Again Tom found himself following her.

'I don't think it's here. It's a mess…' Laura shook her head. 'There's glitter everywhere and…some toys and…oh, I see what's happened.' She straightened up with the bag in her hands. 'My bag fell off the shelf here. Or maybe Harry moved it to find somewhere to put the brick box.' She peered inside the bag. 'Oh, *that's* where that big T Rex got to. It's always been one of Harry's favourites and it's been lost since that day he was in hospital for his pre-surgery MRI scan.'

Suddenly, Laura went very quiet.

'What is it?' Tom asked.

'The glitter…' Laura looked up to catch Tom's gaze and the look in her eyes was heartbreaking. 'There was a card in this bag. Harry had made it for you to say thank you for his dinosaur cap and I was supposed to put it on your desk for a surprise but…but that was the day that gang was in ED and…and it didn't get delivered but it's not in here any more, either.'

It was yet another reminder of how close Tom had become to Laura. That was the day he'd learned about her traumatic past with Harry's father. When that protective instinct had been almost overwhelming and he'd wanted to be the best friend he could be for her and to make sure that nothing awful ever happened to her again.

Well, he hadn't done a very good job of that, had

he? Tom didn't like himself very much in this moment so it came as a surprise to see the way the expression in Laura's eyes changed. Any anger, or maybe it had been sadness, from the way he had deceived her seemed to have evaporated. The mistrust was gone— even the wariness. It looked like hope that she wanted to share. With him.

'I know where he's gone. He is trying to get to the Royal. Not to find Aroha. To find *you*... To give you his card.'

Laura handed the dinosaur toy to Tom and dashed back to the kitchen. She grabbed her phone from the table and then headed straight back to the door.

'You need to stay here,' one of the police officers called. 'In case he finds his way home. We've got plenty of people who can search between here and the hospital. We'll get hospital security onto it, too.'

'He'd hide from anyone like that,' Laura said. 'There's only one person he wants to see and that's Tom.'

He held out his hand as Laura reached him at the door and there was such a wash of relief to be found in the way her hand slipped into his and he could hold it firmly enough to make sure he didn't lose his grip. They were in this together, Tom realised. It felt like this mattered to him as much as it did to Laura.

He'd been an idiot to think that he could make something disappear by ignoring it. It was far too late to avoid the risk that would inevitably be there because of loving either Laura or Harry. The fear he was feeling right now told him exactly what had already happened. This was simply the push that had propelled him towards his own barriers hard enough to shatter them so he couldn't hide any longer. Laura and Harry were *his* people.

His family...

As they turned to head outside, Laura's phone rang. She had to pull her hand from Tom's to answer it but it was hard to make herself do that. The way he was holding on so tightly—the way he'd been looking at her ever since he'd stormed into her kitchen—had made it very clear that something had changed.

Something huge...

She hadn't trusted it. Part of what had caused this whole catastrophe had been what she'd overheard about Tom paying half her rent and the way he'd deceived her and the pain of realising that she'd fallen in love with someone she couldn't trust as much as she'd believed she could.

Had he actually said he was *in* love with her? She hadn't really been listening. She'd lashed out because she was so scared and all she could think about was Harry. But, right now, Laura could see that Tom was as scared as she was. He cared about Harry *that* much. He cared about *her* that much. The connection between them had never felt this powerful but Laura couldn't take the time to try and process what it could mean. There was still only one thing that she could focus on and that was, of course, her precious little boy.

The name on the screen of her phone was surprising.

'Fizz?' Frowning, Laura tilted the phone and Tom bent his head to listen.

'Where are you?' Her friend sounded worried

enough to make Laura think she'd somehow heard about what was going on already.

'I'm at home.'

'Then what the heck is Harry doing here?'

Laura gasped. Her gaze flew up to catch Tom's and for a heartbeat they could share the ultimate relief that Harry was no longer missing. And it was in that moment that Laura could see the absolute truth. The love that was there for both her and Harry. She could hear the echo of his words.

I didn't want to fall in love with you...it happened when I wasn't watching...

A beat of joy morphed with that overwhelming relief but Laura had to push it aside. She would tell Tom exactly how she felt about him later. Much later—when Harry was tucked up safely in his own bed and fast asleep.

'Where's *here*?' she demanded.

'I'm still at work. It was Cooper who spotted Harry, out in the ambulance bay. He's not making much sense, though. He told Cooper you were cross and he doesn't know where Tom's gone and something about a sore tummy. He's upset.'

Again, Laura's gaze snagged Tom's and this time she could see a reflection of her own anxiety that Harry had been telling the truth about feeling unwell. Abdominal pain could be an early sign of things Laura really didn't want to think about.

It was Tom who responded to Fizz this time.

'We're on our way.'

It might have been slightly quicker to get to the hospital on foot but the police officers needed to be sure their assistance was no longer necessary and they

took both Laura and Tom in their car, parking in a des-
ignated slot at one side of the ambulance bay. Laura
didn't let herself think about how Harry had managed
to get across the main road to get here when it was
already almost dark. She couldn't think of anything
other than the need to hold her son in her arms and
make sure that he was okay. Until then, she needed to
hang onto Tom's hand as if she was drowning and he
was keeping her head above water.

She was still holding Tom's hand as they went into
the emergency department. Or rather Tom wasn't letting go of her hand and Fizz wasn't the only staff member to look astonished. Her smile, as she came to meet
them, was both delighted and reassuring.

'Harry's fine,' was the first thing she said. 'He's
with Cooper in the relatives' room.'

But Harry burst into tears the moment he saw his
mother and Laura was in tears herself as she lifted him
to hug him tightly. She heard Cooper saying that he'd
leave them to it as Harry wrapped his arms around her
neck and his legs around her waist, like a little monkey. She knew Tom hadn't left the room with Cooper. She could feel him standing close behind her. So
close it was easy to lean back and the way his arm
came around her shoulders made him instantly part
of this cuddle.

And it felt...

It felt like family...

She had to swallow very hard to try and stop her
tears. 'Is your tummy still sore?' she asked Harry.

'No...'

'So you won't need this fellow, then? To bite anybody?'

The sound of Tom's voice clearly startled Harry. Had he not noticed him coming into the room with her? She could feel the tension in his small body and then he was wriggling to get down from her arms.

Tom must have put that green, plastic T Rex they had found in the hall cupboard in his pocket. He was holding it out now and his question had reminded her of how he'd bonded with Harry from the first moment he'd seen him in the emergency department that day.

Harry remembered, too. He was smiling as he reached up for the toy.

'I made a card for you,' he said. With his other hand, he was pulling a crumpled sheet of paper from his pocket. Glitter sparkled as it rained down onto the floor. 'I drawed T Rex. Mummy forgot to give it to you.'

'I'm sorry about that,' Laura said. 'And I'm sorry I was cross with you today. It wasn't your fault. I was feeling a bit sad, that's all.'

Harry nodded as if he'd known all along. 'Because Tom wasn't at home,' he said, matter-of-factly.

Laura's breath came out in a surprised huff as her gaze flew to meet Tom's. In a way, Harry was right. She'd been devastated because of the increasing distance she could feel between herself and this man that she loved so much and she'd been wondering if he'd ever only been close because he felt sorry for her. He hadn't been "at home" for what felt like a long time.

But he was here now. Totally present. No barriers. He had Harry's card in his hands and there was a glint in his eyes that suggested an unshed tear or two.

'I'll be home from now on,' Tom said, his voice a little raw. 'As much as you want me to be.'

'I want to go home now,' Harry said. 'Will you come and play trains?'

Tom was still holding Laura's gaze. 'If that's okay with Mummy.'

'Mummy?' Harry tugged at Laura's hand. 'Can Tom come home with us now? Is that okay?'

Laura put her hand on the soft fuzz of Harry's new hair but her gaze never left Tom's. How could she look away from that question? That promise?

'It's more than okay,' she said softly. 'Let's go home.'

EPILOGUE

'I HAVE SOMETHING for you.'

'Ooh…' Laura Chapman turned from looking up at the inky night sky studded with stars to raise her eyebrows suggestively at the man who'd come to join her on the veranda of their home. 'Are the kids asleep already?'

Tom was grinning as he sat down on the double swinging chair beside her. 'That can wait.' He bent his head and placed a lingering, tender kiss on her lips. 'For a while, anyway. No…it's this…'

Laura took the small package from his hand. 'A gift? Is it a special occasion I've forgotten about? Oh, no… I don't have a present for you.'

'This is kind of a present for both of us.'

Laura opened the small box. For a moment, she stared at what was inside it, bewildered.

'A pack of cards? When do we ever play cards? Harry might like to learn but the twins are far too young…'

'Take them out,' Tom said. 'Look at the other side of the cards.'

Laura tipped them out of the box and turned them

over. Instead of a normally patterned back, these cards had photographs on the other side.

'It's a kind of thank you,' Tom said softly.

'What for?'

'For changing my life.'

'But what's that got to do with cards? Oh…' Laura pressed her hand to her mouth. 'It's about that time when Harry was first sick, isn't it? When I came into your office and rambled on about the cards that you get dealt in the game of life and having to play the best game you can.' She shook her head. 'How cheesy was that? I was really embarrassed when I thought about it later.'

She picked up one of the cards. The photograph on the back was one of Harry in the oncology day unit. Totally bald but smiling proudly as he pushed his IV pole ahead of him. Laura's smile was poignant. Harry's hair had grown back thicker than ever in the end and it was black and tousled looking. So like Tom's, in fact, that anyone meeting them for the first time would have trouble believing they weren't biological father and son. Or that Harry had ever been sick. Every check-up he'd had since had been clear and they had every reason to hope that they always would be.

'Cheesy enough for me to think about it later myself,' Tom said. 'It made me wonder if I really was playing the best game I could and when I thought about you and the way you were fighting for Harry—loving him that much—it felt like I was awake for the first time in years. Emotionally, anyway. And I felt…lonely. I had no one to fight for. Or to fight for me.'

The photograph Laura was holding now had been

taken at their wedding—well over a year ago now. It had been such a joyous celebration that had taken place in a garden and had included all the most important people in their lives. This particular photograph was of Bella, who had only just learned to walk but was being a flower girl. She had sat down on the grass at this point, however, and Harry was trying to persuade her to hand over the basket so that he could scatter the petals before Harley's fat little fist could remove any more of them.

'I thought you never would want to have people that close again,' Laura said. 'And I totally understood why.' The chair swung gently as she tilted her head to kiss Tom. 'I'm so glad you changed your mind, though.'

'There's a photo of Jenny and Sam on one of the cards. I hope that's okay.'

'Why on earth wouldn't it be? You loved them. They're part of your story so they're part of ours, too. Part of our family.'

Laura breath came out in a huff of laughter as she turned over another card. 'That's the night you proposed to me.'

'And we asked Harry if he remembered what he'd asked for as his special present for being so brave.'

'And he said that he wanted his present wrapped up.'

'And you found all the old paper you had in the cupboard and let him try.'

Laura's smile was misty. She touched the picture with her finger. Tom was lying on the floor with crumpled wrapping paper all over him and Harry had never looked so pleased with himself. She could remember how wonderful that evening had been with so much love between them all.

It was still there. Getting bigger.

She turned over another card.

'There's our house. And me looking the size of a house. How on earth did we think it was a good idea to move when I was six months pregnant with twins?'

'Your apartment was about to burst at the seams. And we'd finally found the perfect house.'

Her apartment. The one Tom had found for her. The one he'd been secretly paying half the rent on. She'd asked him why he'd done that, that night that Harry had run away to find him. That terrifying, amazing night when they had both known they were in love with each other.

'I wanted to protect you,' he'd told her. *'I just didn't want to fall in love with you...but it happened when I wasn't watching...'*

Laura gathered the cards up and snuggled more deeply into Tom's arms. 'You're so right,' she said softly. 'This is a gift for both of us. For all of us.

'And it's a reminder.' Tom pressed a kiss to Laura's hair. 'To play the best game you can. To take risks. If you're not prepared to live with the risk of losing something, that means that you don't have that something. And when it's this good...' He touched Laura's cheek with a soft stroke of his finger that finished on her lips. 'This close to perfect...'

Laura's lips parted, ready for the kiss she knew was coming. 'It's as perfect as it gets, I reckon,' she whispered. 'And we both know that loving anyone is never without risk. But life without love isn't what it should be. I love you so much, Tom.'

'Snap.' Tom's lips were touching hers now. 'It's a card game, you know…'

* * * * *

LET'S TALK
Romance

For exclusive extracts, competitions
and special offers, find us online:

- **f** facebook.com/millsandboon
- **◎** @millsandboonuk
- **𝕏** @millsandboon

Or get in touch on 0844 844 1351*

For all the latest titles coming soon,
visit millsandboon.co.uk/nextmonth